Gr...
To Cup Her Cheek.

He met her gaze and stared deeply into her eyes. He seemed as if he wanted to say something more. Something important.

But, finally, it was Rebecca who broke the silence. "I need to go now. I've stayed way too long...."

He looked sorry to hear she wanted to leave, but his expression quickly turned to one of resignation.

"Yes, of course. You'd better return to your own bed. If anyone finds you here, they might get the right idea about us."

"The *wrong* idea, you mean," she corrected him.

"Oh, right," Grant said, as he leaned over and kissed her softly. "The *wrong* idea. Yes, that's what I meant to say."

Dear Reader,

Escape the winter doldrums by reading six new passionate, powerful and provocative romances from Silhouette Desire!

Start with our MAN OF THE MONTH, *The Playboy Sheikh*, the latest SONS OF THE DESERT love story by bestselling author Alexandra Sellers. Also thrilling is the second title in our yearlong continuity series DYNASTIES: THE CONNELLYS. In *Maternally Yours* by Kathie DeNosky, a pleasure-seeking tycoon falls for a soon-to-be mom.

All you readers who've requested more titles in Cait London's beloved TALLCHIEFS miniseries will delight in her smoldering *Tallchief: The Hunter*. And more great news for our loyal Desire readers—a *brand-new* five-book series featuring THE TEXAS CATTLEMAN'S CLUB, subtitled THE LAST BACHELOR, launches this month. In *The Millionaire's Pregnant Bride* by Dixie Browning, passion erupts between an oil executive and secretary who marry for the sake of her unborn child.

A single-dad surgeon meets his match in *Dr. Desirable*, the second book of Kristi Gold's MARRYING AN M.D. miniseries. And Kate Little's *Tall, Dark & Cranky* is an enchanting contemporary version of *Beauty and the Beast*.

Indulge yourself with all six of these exhilarating love stories from Silhouette Desire!

Enjoy!

Dan Marlow Golan

Joan Marlow Golan
Senior Editor, Silhouette Desire

Please address questions and book requests to:
Silhouette Reader Service
U.S.: 3010 Walden Ave., P.O. Box 1325, Buffalo, NY 14269
Canadian: P.O. Box 609, Fort Erie, Ont. L2A 5X3

Tall, Dark & Cranky
KATE LITTLE

Silhouette® Desire®

Published by Silhouette Books
America's Publisher of Contemporary Romance

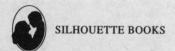 SILHOUETTE BOOKS

ISBN 0-373-76422-7

TALL, DARK & CRANKY

Copyright © 2002 by Anne Canadeo

Visit Silhouette at www.eHarlequin.com

Printed in U.S.A.

Books by Kate Little

Silhouette Desire

Jingle Bell Baby #1043
Husband for Keeps #1276
The Determined Groom #1302
The Millionaire Takes a Bride #1349
The Bachelorette #1401
Tall, Dark & Cranky #1422

KATE LITTLE

claims to have lots of experience with romance—"the *fictional* kind, that is," she is quick to clarify. She has been both an author and an editor of romance fiction for over fifteen years. She believes that a good romance will make the reader experience all the tension, thrills and agony of falling madly, deeply and wildly in love. She enjoys watching the characters in her books go crazy for each other, but hates to see the blissful couple disappear when it's time for them to live happily ever after. In addition to writing romance novels, Kate also writes fiction and nonfiction for young adults. She lives on Long Island, New York, with her husband and daughter.

One

———

"**Y**our recommendations are impressive, Ms. Calloway. In fact, they were positively glowing. One of your former employers even called you a miracle worker," Matthew Berringer said.

"I love my work and I'm good at it," Rebecca said in her usual straightforward fashion. "But I'd hardly call myself a miracle worker."

"You wouldn't, eh? That's too bad, because I'm not sure that anything short of a miracle will restore my brother Grant, to his former life. To any sort of productive life at all."

She saw instantly that her reply had dampened Matthew Berringer's enthusiasm, and Rebecca wondered if she should have been more…diplomatic. She could have soft-soaped her answer a bit. She'd been warned that her pungent honesty was sometimes a shortcoming. Rebecca bit her lower lip. She needed this job. But she wouldn't be hired on false impressions and she would never make any false promises.

She knew how demanding, physically and emotionally, a home assignment like this one might be. From what she'd heard about the patient, she wasn't sure she'd succeed in rehabilitating him, much less getting him up and about his business by the summer's end, which was Matthew Berringer's explicit request. She wasn't sure anyone could. From what she'd seen in the medical records, the problem wasn't so much Grant Berringer's physical condition as his attitude.

Miracle worker, indeed. All the Berringers' money and then some couldn't buy a miracle. And Rebecca knew she couldn't live up to such high-flown accolades...and didn't want to break her heart trying.

"Mr. Berringer, your concern for your brother is very touching. He's fortunate to have someone so involved in his recovery—"

"Your kind words seem to be leading up to something, Ms. Calloway." Matthew Berringer interrupted her. "Perhaps you should just say it?"

Rebecca was taken aback, then found his frankness refreshing. There *was* something more she wanted to say.

"You can't will your brother to get well again, to resume a productive life, if he doesn't want to. You can hire a hundred therapists. Even some that *will* promise you miracles. But no one can snap their fingers and give your brother the will to fight his way back. He has to want it. He has to want it very badly.''

He stared at her, looking angry at her words, she thought. Or at least greatly irritated. Then, without replying, he looked at her résumé and letters of reference again, as if reviewing the pages for final questions.

She'd blown it totally, Rebecca realized. She wasn't going to get this job. She could always tell when the interviewer started studying her résumé in the middle of everything. She predicted he would soon lift his head, bestow a dismissing smile and send her off with some polite comment that would let her know she was low on the list.

Rebecca glanced at her surroundings. She'd been so intent on answering Matthew Berringer's questions, she hadn't taken much notice of the room. Sunny and spacious, it appeared to be a library or study. The walls were lined with floor-to-ceiling bookcases, and the furnishings were large, comfortably worn pieces upholstered in leather and tapestry fabrics. There were many framed photos. Some looked quite old. Most looked like family groups.

Area rugs in traditional designs covered the polished wooden floor, and an impressive carved oak desk stood in front of glass doors that led to a covered terrace. The doors stood ajar, allowing the spring air to fill the room.

When the interview began, she'd expected Matthew Berringer to take a seat behind the big desk. Instead, he'd sat on a couch across from her and offered her coffee from a silver service. The gesture, though small, had helped put her at ease.

She took a moment to raise her china cup and take a sip. The coffee was cold, but at least it gave her something to do.

In the tense silence, Rebecca could hear the ocean, just steps away from the terrace of the beachfront property. The steady rhythm of the waves was soothing and helped her relax.

It was a pity she wasn't going to work here. The Berringer mansion—merely Grant Berringer's summer home—was so beautiful, the kind of grand old place she'd so far only admired from a wistful distance. Earlier Matthew Berringer had told her a little about the estate, which was set on ten acres of oceanfront property. The twelve-bedroom mansion, designed in the style of a French Norman manor house, was built in the 1920s for a wealthy oil magnate, part of New York's aristocracy. The stones had been shipped from Europe, as well as the craftsmen who had put the place together. The carved stone architectural details included gargoyles with all too human faces. With its wide, rambling structure, courtyards, slate roof and turrets, the place looked more like a miniature castle, Rebecca thought, nestled in a grove of woods near the sea. The decor within was fit for royalty, as well.

Not only did she need a new job, but she and Nora, her six-year-old daughter, needed a new place to live by the end of the month and an apartment in one wing of the huge house was part of the deal, in addition to a generous salary. Matthew Berringer had already shown her the rooms, which were lovely. Certainly enough space for her and Nora for the summer. If Grant Berringer required her services for longer than the summer and Nora had to return to school, Rebecca had told Matthew Berringer some other arrangements would be necessary. But he hadn't seemed put off by that potential complication. He'd stated that he'd be happy to hire a tutor for Nora or enroll her in one of the fancy private schools nearby. Rebecca felt satisfied by his reply. Although she had read Grant Berringer's medical records and discussed his condition with Matthew, she still needed to see him with her own eyes to gauge how long he would need her help.

Living on the beach for the summer, in such luxurious surroundings, no less, would have been heavenly. But…she'd blown it all with her irrepressible need to be honest.

Well, she wasn't really sorry. She'd only told Matthew Berringer the truth. People always say they admire honesty. In theory, perhaps, but not in actuality, she'd noticed. Not in her case, anyway. Perhaps she'd helped him, in a way. He'd be wary of the next applicant, who might claim to be able to have Grant Berringer behind his desk in no time flat.

Finally, Matthew Berringer looked at her. The irritation in his expression had disappeared.

"I know what you've told me is true, Ms. Calloway. I know the real motivation has to come from within Grant. I just don't want to believe it, I guess. I keep wishing I might find someone who could snap their fingers and make my brother well again," he admitted.

"I understand. I really do," she sympathized. "Just about everyone I meet who is caring for a loved one feels the same."

"But my brother's case is different from most you've had in the past," Matthew Berringer said. "He has had an extraordinary loss. Many people use the word tragedy when they're describing a sad but not necessarily unusual event. My brother, however, has lived through a tragedy, a devastating event that cost him…everything. And left him with an impossibly heavy burden of guilt, in the bargain."

So far, Rebecca had only learned that Grant Berringer had been in a car accident. She'd heard that he'd been the driver and there was one passenger involved who had died instantly. Grant had escaped with multiple injuries the most severe to his right hip and leg. Those were the basic facts, but obviously there was more to the story.

"Why don't you tell me everything about your brother's accident? Everything you think is relevant to his recovery, I mean. I do need to know the complete details in order to evaluate the case."

Loss was something she knew about. She could empathize with Grant Berringer. But at the same time, she had been through so much in her life, Rebecca wasn't sure she had the resources to handle an unusually demanding assignment.

Matthew Berringer's cool blue-eyed gaze met hers, then he looked away. It seemed he was gathering his thoughts. "I'll try to keep this brief and to the point," he said. "My brother was engaged to be married. He and his fiancée, Courtney Benton, were returning to the city after spending the weekend at the country home of one of my brother's clients. It was bad weather, a sudden heavy rainstorm, and my brother apparently lost control of the wheel. The car skidded off the road and crashed into a cement wall. Courtney was killed instantly. My brother was in a coma for two weeks. When he woke up and learned what had happened, he barely had the will to go on living.''

"Oh, dear…that is heartbreaking," Rebecca said softly. She had heard many sad stories during her career, but this was one of the saddest. That poor man. She couldn't imagine his grief…or his guilt.

"And to complicate matters even further, my brother has some memory loss. He can recall events leading up to the accident. Leaving the home they were visiting and such. But he can't remember anything that happened right before the crash occurred. He can't even remember if he and Courtney were trying to pull over and wait out the rain.''

Matthew Berringer sounded amazed but somewhat frustrated. "The doctors say he may never remember.''

"They may be right," Rebecca agreed. "I have heard of such situations before. It's a reaction to extreme trauma or stress. It's the mind's way of protecting itself from memories that are too painful to relive.''

"Yes, I understand all that." As Matthew Berringer nodded, a lock of his smooth brown hair dropped across his brow, and he impatiently brushed it back. "But I often suspect that if Grant could remember all that happened that night—no matter how distressing those memories might be—perhaps he'd be able to move forward, to work through his grief and rebuild his life.''

"Yes, it might help him a great deal. But it's a catch-22 of sorts, isn't it?'' she added. "He *will* get stronger if he remembers. But he'll only be ready to remember when he gets stronger.''

"It's a riddle inside a riddle.'' Matthew shook his head, and Rebecca could sense his frustration and sadness. Matthew had also experienced a loss, she realized. The loss of a brother who was once vital and strong, an equal in friendship and camaraderie, for it was clear that the two were quite close.

Rebecca did not know how to reply and thought it best to say nothing. Sometimes it helped people to talk, even if she couldn't supply an easy answer. She sensed that Matthew Berringer needed to talk right now to someone he thought could understand not only his brother's dilemma, but his own, as well. "So you see, if he's fallen into some dark pit of despair and is reluctant to return to the land of living, I believe, that after all he's been through, it's an understandable reaction.''

"Completely understandable.'' Rebecca nodded and looked at her hands, which were folded in her lap.

Now that she knew the tragic story, she could see why Matthew was looking for a therapist who might be part superhero, part saint. The question loomed even larger—was she the right person for this job?

"I know the will to return must come from him,'' he added, echoing her earlier words, "but I was hoping—praying, if you must know—that I could find the right...messenger. Someone who understands such matters and is willing to go down into that dark place and convince him to come back to us.''

His voice, which had been calm, increased in emotion, so that finally, Rebecca was quite moved by Matthew Berringer's caring speech.

He was an uncommonly good man, she thought. A kind man. The type who would never give up on someone he loved. Rebecca admired that. Yet, despite his striking good looks and admirable qualities, she did not feel the least bit attracted to him.

It was funny how that worked, Rebecca reflected. The chemistry was either there...or it wasn't. In this case, it clearly wasn't. Not for him, either, she suspected. She could tell these things by now. Though he seemed to respect her professionally and to like her well enough in a friendly way. Which was all for the better, she thought, if he was possibly to be her employer.

''I'd like you to meet my brother. Will you come with me now and talk to him?''

''Yes, of course.'' Rebecca was surprised at the invitation. Then pleased. She usually wasn't asked to meet the patient if the interview was a total loss. Perhaps there was more hope of being hired here than she thought.

Besides, she was curious to meet Grant Berringer. It would help them both to decide if she was right for the job.

Matthew led her through the elegantly decorated mansion, and Rebecca quickly peeked through doorways and admired her surroundings. The house was furnished with a mixture of antiques and traditionally designed pieces, with sumptuous drapery, original art-work and interesting porcelain and statuary. Yet the decor didn't look at all stuffy or museumlike. The rooms retained a fresh, light-filled look Rebecca found inviting.

"Grant has a few rooms upstairs, but when he was released from the hospital, the doctors advised me to set him up on the ground floor. I fixed a suite of rooms for him in the west wing of the house, including an exercise room with all types of equipment for his therapy. I'm in the city during the week, but I've hired a private nurse to take care of him during the day. A young man named Joe Newton. He's been great with Grant, very patient."

While most health-care professionals needed to extend patience to their charges, Rebecca sensed Grant Berringer required an extraordinary effort in that respect. *Not* a good sign.

"Our housekeeper, Miriam Walker, lives in," Matthew continued. "There's an intercom system throughout the house, so Grant can call her if there's any need."

Rebecca listened and nodded. It sounded as if Matthew had thought of everything. They had passed several large main rooms—a banquet-size dining room, an impressive parlor and a huge kitchen stocked with professional-looking cooking equipment. Lured by the view, Rebecca couldn't help but slow her step to glance inside the doorway.

"Great kitchen," she remarked when Matthew turned to glance at her.

He smiled. "You must like to cook if the sight of all those pots and pans and gadgetry turns you on."

"I do. When I have the time." She thought of the tiny, ill-equipped kitchen in her apartment in the city. It was a challenge, but she still managed to turn out some great meals for dinner guests or for herself and Nora when she had the time and inspiration to experiment. What a treat it would be to cook in a kitchen like this one.

"It's a very relaxing hobby, I hear," Matthew said. "Never caught my interest, though. I much prefer to work out my frustrations on a golf course…then visit a good restaurant for dinner," he joked. "But my brother loves to cook. He had just had the kitchen redone before the accident. He was quite a chef. He had so many interests—tennis, sailing, skiing, traveling to the most exotic places. He played hard and worked hard. He's known on Wall Street, too. Notorious, in fact, for being tough, even ruthless, some say. Grant is a successful, self-made man who knows how to live life to the fullest. Or did, before the accident," Matthew added. "You couldn't guess it, though, to see him now."

"He could be that way again," she said optimistically. "In time."

"Yes, I suppose," he agreed with a heavy sigh. "But it's hard to believe when you see him now."

They had arrived at double doors at the end of a long hall. Matthew knocked once, and a male voice answered. "Just a moment."

A young man with short dark hair answered the door. Joe Newton, the private nurse, Rebecca assumed. He smiled at Rebecca in greeting. He had a kind, gentle manner, she thought, if first impressions were any clue. He looked quite strong, as well. Was Grant Berringer so incapacitated that he required a weight lifter's aid? From what she'd read of his injuries, it shouldn't be as dire as all that.

Matthew led her into the room and made some quick introductions.

"How's Grant doing this afternoon?" Beneath Matthew's casual tone, Rebecca could sense his concern.

Joe shrugged a hefty shoulder. "About the same, I'd say. I persuaded him to go out on the beach after breakfast, then he wanted a nap. He refused to do any exercise today. Said his hip hurt too much," Joe reported with a frown. "He's been resting for some time now. I was just about to try to get him up."

A nap, in the middle of a day like this one? His depression was deep. While she had a degree in psychology as well as one in physiotherapy, she wondered if she was professionally equipped to treat this man.

"Let me go into him alone first," Matthew said.

Matthew disappeared into the adjoining room and Rebecca was left alone with Joe. "Are you interviewing as a physical therapist?" he asked her.

Rebecca nodded. "Have there been many others here so far?"

"Matthew has hired plenty. But they don't last

very long. Grant scares them away,'' Joe replied with a laugh.

Matthew Berringer had neglected to add that tidbit of information during their talk, Rebecca realized. Perhaps her chances of getting this job weren't as bad as she thought.

"I don't scare easily," Rebecca told Joe with a smile.

"He's tough," the nurse assured her. "I try to help him as much as I can. To get his strength back and such. But he prefers me to be more of a glorified baby-sitter.''

"Matthew said you were patient with him. He appreciates that," Rebecca confided.

"I try to be." She could see that the compliment had touched him. "Grant's a good guy underneath it all. I'd like to see him get back to his old self.''

It seems everyone who knew Grant shared the same hope, Rebecca reflected. Then she heard Matthew's voice. "Ms. Calloway, could you come in here, please?''

"Be right there," she replied. She turned away from Joe and began walking to the open doorway.

"Good luck," he whispered as she passed. She simply smiled in reply. She didn't know why she felt such a fluttering in her stomach. She was never nervous about meeting prospective patients.

She entered the room slowly. It seemed very dark and stuffy, considering the weather outside. Her eyes took a moment to adjust to the dim light, then she could still see that the place was a mess, with books and newspapers scattered about, a tray of food that looked barely picked over and an unmade bed in the midst of everything. Considering the appearance of the rest of the house, she could only assume that Grant Berringer preferred his personal area to be left in such a state.

Some distance from the doorway, she could make out Matthew's tall form, and beside him a man in a wheelchair who she assumed was Grant. His back was turned to her. Not a good sign, she thought.

As she walked toward them, Rebecca's first instinct was to pull open the long curtains that covered one wall. From the layout of the adjoining room, she guessed the drapery covered glass doors that led to the long deck and framed an ocean view. Some sunlight and fresh air would do a world of good in here, she thought.

But she didn't touch the curtains. Instead, she continued to approach the two men. Matthew's voice cut through the tense silence.

"Ms. Calloway, I'd like you to meet my brother Grant." His tone was so smooth and sociable, Rebecca thought she might have stumbled into a garden party instead of this dark, stuffy lair.

"I would like to meet him," Rebecca replied, standing just a few feet from them. "If he'd be so kind as to turn around."

Matthew looked at Grant, a tense expression on his face. But he didn't say anything. They waited what seemed a long time, though it was perhaps only a moment or two.

Then finally Grant Berringer spun his wheelchair around and Rebecca had her first look at him. His hair was dark and thick. Appealingly so, she thought. She couldn't tell if he was growing a beard or had just neglected to shave for a day or two. His cheeks had a scruffy appearance that could not detract from his strong good looks. With his hair combed straight back from his forehead and his broad, high cheekbones and angular jaw, his face had a distinctly regal, lionlike appearance.

He was extremely attractive, she thought, though not in a smooth, typical way, the way his brother, Matthew, was handsome.

She'd learned the basic facts of his physical appearance from his medical records—six feet in height, one hundred and seventy-five pounds. At thirty-eight years old, he was almost ten years her senior. Yet the basic facts had not prepared her for some undefinable quality he possessed—his sheer intensity, which was as much a characteristic of the man as the dark eyes that took her in from head to toe.

"You'll forgive me for not getting up." He greeted her in a gruff, sarcastic voice.

His eyes, framed by thick brows, looked large and luminous in the dimly lit room. The rugged lines of his face held a serious, almost angry expression.

"No apology necessary," Rebecca replied lightly. "Of course, considering your condition, Mr. Berringer, you could be out of that chair by now, you know."

"You think so, do you?" he challenged her. He gave a bitter laugh, then turned to his brother. "Did you find yet *another* Mary Poppins for the job, Matthew?" His voice sounded weary and vaguely amused. "One would think the supply would be exhausted by now."

"One would think your brother would be exhausted by now, trying to help you, Mr. Berringer," Rebecca replied quietly.

She saw Matthew Berringer's eyebrows pop up at her tart response. But he said nothing. Grant finally lifted his head and stared into her eyes. He seemed impressed. Almost animated. She gave herself two points for that achievement, anyway.

"Well, well...this one's got some spunk, I'll give her that much," he said to Matthew. Rebecca thought she'd noticed a spark of appreciation in his eyes as he gazed at her, then thought she must have been mistaken. His gaze remained flat and dispassionate. "I've always preferred a tart, cool taste myself, as opposed to something sticky and overly sweet."

"None of my patients ever accused me of being too sweet," Rebecca replied. "More like the opposite."

"I'm not your *patient* yet, Ms. Calloway," he reminded her harshly. "Not by a long shot."

Rebecca was taken aback, but only for a moment. The wounded lion, cornered in his den, she thought. All he could do was give a loud roar and hope to scare the intruder away.

There was a small chair near his wheelchair, and she walked over and sat in it. She knew that being on the same eye level as the patient—not staring down at them—should help ease a tense moment like this one.

"You're right. My mistake," she said simply.

He stared directly at her, and she had her first good look at him, up close and personal. Intimidating was the word that first came to mind. But as she gazed unflinchingly into his dark eyes, she saw his vulnerability, as well, and the wellspring of pain and fear that had driven him to this dark place.

A thin white scar extended from the corner of his eye to his jawline, marring one cheek. Rebecca had read in the medical report that Grant could have easily had the scar erased with plastic surgery, but for some reason preferred not to. Did he keep it to help him mourn his loss? Or as a penance he felt bound to pay?

Her heart was touched by him, moved by him. Not by pity or compassion, exactly, but by some inexplicable urge to restore him, physically and spiritually, to siphon into him some of her abundant strength and will.

She had never felt quite this reaction to a prospective patient before, Rebecca thought with a mental jolt. Why this one?

Then suddenly, Grant's voice broke into her thoughts.

"I like a person who can admit when they're wrong," he said in a low, deep voice.

"I do a lot of that," she admitted. "Maybe you'll end up liking me, after all."

He suddenly laughed, and the deep, warm sound skimmed along her nerve endings, lighting a path in its wake—a reaction that alarmed Rebecca and one she forced herself to ignore. Still, she couldn't ignore the sudden change in Grant Berringer's appearance. His smile was like a sudden burst of light exploding in the shadowy room. His face was transformed, soft-ened, making his dark good looks even more appeal-ing, Rebecca thought, as her gaze lingered on the small, attractive lines fanning from the corners of his eyes and deep dimples beside a full, sensual mouth.

Rebecca quickly pulled her gaze away. What was going on here? Was she attracted to him?

No, it couldn't be. *Mustn't* be. She'd been warned about this but it had never happened to her. She tried to find some rational reason it would happen now. It was his sad story, she told herself. Matthew had drawn Grant as a tragic—even romantic—figure. The story had gotten to her. It had to be. She couldn't compromise her professional standards by taking on a case when she had a romantic interest in the patient.

As if reading her mind, Grant said, "You know, Ms. Calloway, there are women, like yourself, who have come here hoping to bag a rich husband. If that's your intention, I may as well warn you now, you'd be wasting your time."

Rebecca knew his insult was merely a tactic, a ploy to drive her away, but it stung nonetheless to hear her ethics—and those of her colleagues—disparaged.

"Grant, please," Matthew urged his brother. "Why do you have to do this?"

Matthew had been quiet until now. He seemed to think Rebecca and his brother should sort things out, and she was grateful for that. She could hear his frus-tration and embarrassment for Grant's rudeness.

"No, it's okay," she assured Matthew. She turned to Grant again. "Mr. Berringer, I can promise you, the last thing in the world I'm looking for is a husband, rich or otherwise.''

She watched him blink in surprise, but he showed no other reaction to her words.

''All right, point taken,'' he replied. He paused, then looked at her. ''My brother says you're highly qualified. The best he's found so far. But I want you to give me one good reason I should hire you for this job. Especially when so many others before have clearly failed at it. One good reason, Ms. Calloway,'' he added, the note of challenge in his voice growing sharper. ''That's all I'm asking for.''

Rebecca sat straight in her chair. She was being tested, like some character in a myth, required to answer the riddle before a magic portal to another realm would open or some treasure would be handed over.

She wasn't sure what she should say or do, and on a sudden impulse, she stood and pulled open the heavy curtains. Sunlight flooded the room. God, she'd been itching to do that since she'd come in.

From the corner of her eye, she could see Grant Berringer reel back in his chair, one arm raised to shield his eyes from the sudden flash of light. Rebecca ignored his reaction.

''Here, come with me a minute, I want to show you something.'' Without waiting for Grant's reply, she flipped off the brakes of his chair and quickly wheeled him toward the open glass door.

''What are you doing?'' he demanded. ''Have you lost your mind?''

''Maybe. But that doesn't mean I'm not a nice person,' Rebecca answered lightly as she pushed his chair onto the deck. Inside the room, she could hear Matthew softly chuckling. She pushed Grant's chair to the middle of the balcony, near the railing.

"That was quite a ride," Grant said. "You're stronger than you look."

"Strong enough to handle you," she promised.

He grunted something in reply, but Rebecca couldn't make out any distinct words. The sound of his dismay made her smile.

"So why have you brought me out here, Ms. Calloway? To catch pneumonia, maybe?"

"It's not that cold," she countered with a laugh. "It's not cold at all."

"Or maybe you plan to push me off the balcony? Put me out of my misery?"

His words were spoken in a jesting tone, but they touched an alarm in Rebecca. She knew his cynical joke came from a deep, frightening place, and she knew with almost utter certainty that Grant Berringer had considered ending his life, perhaps in that very manner. Still, she managed to answer him in a joking tone.

"I've rarely been known to push a patient off a balcony. On purpose, I mean," she said casually. "And I certainly wouldn't choose such a low one," she added, peering over the edge to the beach below. "I'd definitely take you up to the second or third floor for something like that."

"Thanks, I feel much better now," he said. Rebecca restrained herself from laughing. "That still doesn't answer my question, though. Why are we out here, Ms. Calloway?"

"For the view, of course," she replied, as if he should have guessed. "It's breathtaking, isn't it?"

Rebecca stood straight and took a deep breath. The ocean air was wonderful. And the view of the water and the blue sky above… Well, they reminded her of how great it was just to be alive. Couldn't he feel that, too?

"Oh, that." He dismissed her enthusiasm with a sarcastic laugh. "You get used to it. Believe me."

"I never would," she countered. She moved around his chair and stood beside him.

He glanced at her, then at the horizon. "Yes, you're the type who probably wouldn't," he said quietly. "But most people do. Besides, you still haven't given me a reason to give you the job."

Rebecca felt suddenly nervous, anxious. This wasn't working out as she had expected. He was tough. Maybe too tough for her?

She stood behind him again, and on impulse covered his eyes with her hands. His skin felt warm to her touch, and she could feel his entire body grow tense and alert. Yet he didn't roar a protest, as she expected. Or try to pull away. She felt his brow furrow in a puzzled frown. Then his large hands came up to cover hers.

"What are you doing now, playing peekaboo? The woman is mad, definitely," he murmured to himself.

Rebecca ignored his complaint. "I know you're used to the view, take it for granted, in fact. But what if you couldn't see the ocean ever again. How would you feel about that?"

"It wouldn't matter to me one bit. I don't really

see it now," he confessed in a flat voice. "I don't deserve to see it at any rate."

Her heart clenched at his words. Yes, it all came down to his guilt. He wouldn't allow himself to reach out for life again. He believed he didn't deserve it. He was trying to punish himself—and scare off anyone who tried to stop him from punishing himself.

She took her hands off his eyes, yet for some inexplicable reason, her hands floated down to trace the line of his lightly bearded cheeks. With the fingertips of her right hand, she felt the thin ridge of his scar, and a wave of emotion for him washed through her as she lifted her hands.

His hands did not prevent her from moving, but they held her, transmitting a sense that he was reluctant to feel her break contact.

But she did break contact and stood behind his chair with her arms dangling at her sides, her body feeling subtly charged from the brief touch.

"I'd like to say I understand," she said quietly. "But I'm sure you believe that nobody really can."

"Very wise. I don't see how anyone could."

Standing behind Grant Berringer, she couldn't see his face. But his voice was filled with emotion, the most she'd heard from him so far.

She paused and took a deep breath. She was losing him. Not just losing her chance at getting the job. But losing her chance to help this man who had mysteriously touched something within her. She suddenly wanted to be the one to help him. She suddenly believed she could succeed where all the others had failed.

She moved to face him. "I took you out here because I thought that the sight of this beautiful day would remind you it's simply great to be alive. And that's the best reason to want to recover."

"Spare me, Ms. Calloway. I've heard all these little sermons before."

"Yes, I'm sure you have. But maybe we're both right. It doesn't have to be one way or the other, you know."

"I don't quite get your meaning."

"Well, if what I'm saying is true, maybe you think that means your loss is without value. That what you've been through isn't truly important. But that's not what I mean at all," she assured him. "If you allow yourself to look at the ocean, Mr. Berringer, and truly see it again and wonder at the sheer power and beauty of it…well, that's okay," she said quietly. "It doesn't diminish your loss or make your pain meaningless. If you choose to go on with your life and build yourself up again, physically and emotionally, it doesn't erase the past or make you disloyal to the memory of your fiancée."

He held her gaze for a moment, then looked away, smoothing his hair with his hand. He seemed disturbed by her speech, and Rebecca braced herself for a tirade. Then he appeared to settle into his own thoughts as he stared at the sea. She wondered what those thoughts were. She couldn't begin to guess.

He had a strong profile, she noticed, one that spoke of determination, even a stubborn streak. If looks were any indication, maybe he'd make it, after all.

"I'll take you back in now," she offered after a

few moments. "Unless of course you'd like to stay out here alone for a while?"

"I can get myself back in, when I'm damned good and ready," he replied curtly. "But is the interview over, Ms. Calloway?" he asked, his tone mockingly polite. "I thought that small formality was the employer's prerogative."

Rebecca suppressed a laugh. "My mistake...once again."

"Yes, that's two. But who's counting? Frankly, I'm amazed that I'm still interested in hiring you at all."

"Yes, so am I," she replied honestly, feeling her heartbeat quicken at his words.

"So...do you want the job or not?" he asked impatiently.

Her immediate impulse was to answer "Yes." But she restrained herself.

"I'm glad you want to hire me, Mr. Berringer. But I do need to think it over for a day or so. I hope that's acceptable to you."

"As you wish. You can call Matthew with your decision," he instructed.

"All right, I'll do that," she replied. Had she hurt his feelings when she didn't accept right away? He was pouting like a small boy. Well, she couldn't help that.

"Did I scare you?" he asked suddenly. His black eyes were narrowed in a brooding look that had already become familiar to her. "You hardly seem the timid type."

"No, not at all," she called over her shoulder. "You'll have to try much harder if I come back."

"Yes, I will try harder. I'll be absolutely impossible," he promised. "See, you've motivated me already."

Rebecca met his glance quickly then continued on her way. His brief smile was heart-stopping. Both a good sign...and bad, she thought with dismay. She kept going, through the glass door, through Grant's messy bedroom to the outer room, where she found Matthew waiting for her.

"How did it go?" Matthew asked eagerly, rising from his chair.

"All right, I suppose. He offered me the job."

"That's great!" Matthew smiled, and his blue eyes lit with pleasure. "When can you start?" he asked eagerly.

"Well, I haven't accepted yet. I need some time to think it over. A day or two, at the most. Your brother told me I should call you with my answer."

"Yes, call me with your answer as soon as you decide, Ms. Calloway. And if there are any questions, any questions at all—about the salary or living arrangements—please know I'll do all I can to make the situation comfortable for you."

Rebecca promised she would call as soon as she came to a decision, and Matthew showed her to the front door, where they said goodbye.

As Rebecca started up her car and drove down the long driveway toward the main road, she wondered why she hadn't accepted on the spot. While she dithered, the Berringers might interview someone else and offer them the position. The salary they'd spoken of was very generous. As were the extras. It was a plum assignment, really. Except for one thing. The patient.

Grant Berringer hadn't scared her. But her feelings and reactions to him certainly had.

Two

Although Rebecca had expected to deliberate over the job offer for at least a day or more, she could think of nothing else during the long drive back to the city. By the time she arrived at the front door to her apartment in a brownstone building on Manhattan's Upper West Side, she had more or less decided that she had no real choice at all. She felt compelled to accept, despite a niggling, intuitive warning that the job would be a hard one, perhaps the hardest she'd ever faced.

Yet each time she'd pondered turning it down, the vision of Grant Berringer's dark, luminous eyes and bleak, haunted expression would rise before her, and she'd feel herself swaying again toward a positive answer.

Rebecca had faced some hard cases but prided herself on the fact that she had never failed to inspire her patients to work hard and heal. She had a solid reputation in her field—which was why Matthew Berringer had gotten in touch with her in the first place. Did she dare put that professional reputation on the line for a man she barely knew—and didn't even necessarily like? If she failed with a well-known man like Grant Berringer—and joined the ranks of his rejected therapists—the word would soon get around. It might make it difficult to find another assignment.

Well then, she couldn't fail, could she? Somehow, she had to break through the fortress he'd built around his wounded heart and soul. The injuries to his body were serious but irrelevant, Rebecca believed. It was the inner man who needed to recover. And once that began to happen, the rest would follow easily, as night follows day.

Rebecca quickly changed from her interview suit into comfortable, worn jeans and a striped T-shirt. With a tall cold drink in hand, she dialed Matthew Berringer. He sounded surprised to hear from her. But when she accepted the offer, he seemed so pleased and grateful, Rebecca felt she'd made the right choice, after all. She arranged to move into the Berringer mansion the following weekend, which was right after Nora's last day of school.

Since her stay would be temporary, Matthew insisted on paying her moving expenses and any unexpected costs, such as rent on her apartment or storage for furniture. While Rebecca appreciated his consideration and concern, she had been asked to move out of her apartment at the end of the month to give way to the landlord's brother. And as for items to put in storage, since her divorce, she and Nora had been traveling light, and Rebecca thought she could fit most of their belongings in the back of her Jeep Cherokee.

"Grant will be very pleased to hear the news," Matthew said. "He was impressed by your meeting."

"Yes, I'm sure," Rebecca replied, smiling. "The same way a bored cat is impressed with a particularly feisty mouse."

"Well...that, too," Matthew conceded with a laugh. "But I think he's finally met a worthy adversary. My money is riding on you, Rebecca."

Rebecca thanked him for the vote of confidence. They discussed the terms of her contract and ended the conversation on a cheerful note. The moment she hung up the phone, however, she felt a knot of dread in the pit of her stomach. Well, she'd accepted. The contract would arrive in a few days, and once she signed it, she was committed to the assignment.

Rebecca shoved worrisome thoughts aside and began making a list of all she had to do in the next week to prepare for the move. She looked up to see that it was time to pick up Nora at school, a task that was performed by a sitter while Rebecca was working. But Rebecca liked to meet her daughter whenever she was able.

Nora greeted her with a giant hug. They walked down the tree-lined street toward home hand in hand while Nora chatted happily about her adventures of the day. With the school year coming to a close, the teachers were clearly growing weary, and the children

were getting wilder every day. Rebecca was barely
able to interrupt Nora's conversation long enough to
offer her some ice cream at a favorite shop. They sat
at the counter and each ordered their usual flavor,
strawberry for Rebecca and Rocky Road for Nora.
Once Nora had settled down, Rebecca told her about
her new job and explained that they'd be moving to
the patient's house for the summer.

"You mean, like when we stay at Grammy's, in
the guest room?" Nora asked, sounding puzzled.

Rebecca had to smile at the comparison. Her
mother lived in a lovely old Victorian house on the
Connecticut shore, the house where Rebecca had been
raised along with two sisters. But the entire home
would fit quite neatly into the space of the Berringers'
east wing, she thought.

"Not quite like Grammy's guest room. We'll have
our own private apartment, about the size of the apartment we have now. But it will be part of the Berringers' house," Rebecca explained. "Their house is
very large. The kind you call a mansion."

Nora's lovely little face was still puckered in a
frown. "Oh, you mean sort of like a castle?"

"Well...not exactly. But a little like a castle, I
guess," Rebecca conceded, taking a spoonful of ice
cream. There *was* a genuine, fire-breathing dragon on
the premises, she reflected.

Nora seemed satisfied by that answer and excited
to be living at the beach. Rebecca realized she would
have to enroll Nora in a day camp or some type of
summer program so her daughter would be occupied

during working hours, but Rebecca was sure she would easily find something suitable.

"I think Eloise will love living in a castle," Nora said. "Maybe she'll learn how to swim."

Oh, dear, the cat, Rebecca thought. She'd almost forgotten about Eloise. But the cat, who had been with Nora since she was only two, couldn't be left behind. She'd have to tell Matthew Berringer about Eloise, of course, and hope he didn't mind.

"Cats don't like water much, Nora," Rebecca reminded her. "But I'm sure she won't complain about seafood dinners."

Nora laughed. As they walked home, Rebecca felt relieved that her daughter had taken the news of their sudden move so easily. Some other children would have been upset about the unexpected change. But Nora had always had an easy temperament, even as a baby. She'd always taken changes in stride, too. Even the breakup of their little family. Nora had only been four years old when Rebecca's husband had asked for a divorce, claiming he'd fallen madly in love with a co-worker.

Rebecca had been crushed by the betrayal, but not truly surprised. In the years since Nora's arrival, it seemed that she and her husband, Jack, had been growing increasingly distant and they spent little time together as a couple—except to argue about money, or Jack's late nights out with his pals, or all the day-to-day problems in every married life. But while Rebecca had noticed the change in their relationship and wondered how to rekindle their romantic spark, she'd never imagined that Jack had found someone else.

She'd never once considered being unfaithful to him. No matter what.

They had been sweethearts since high school, and his disloyalty was a great blow to her. Still, for Nora's sake, Rebecca had offered to forgive and forget, if Jack was willing to end his affair and try to work on their marriage. She was even willing to recognize that she had played some part in his seeking passion elsewhere.

But Jack had claimed it was too late and any efforts in that direction would be useless. He also claimed that he loved her...but not the way a man should love his wife. Maybe they'd married too young, or simply knew each other too long and too well. While it all sounded like the typical excuses of an unfaithful spouse, Rebecca knew there was some truth to his words. Maybe she *had* always been too devoted to Jack, her love and loyalty too easily won. His great romance hadn't held together very long, but that, too, was predictable, Rebecca realized.

The blow was awesome, but it was a clean break and irrevocable. As painful as it had been to face the truth, her loving feelings for Jack had withered and grown cold soon after she'd learned about his deception. In fact, in the passing years, she'd come to see him differently. It wasn't just bitterness, either, she knew. While they were married, she'd accepted and overlooked his immaturity and self-centered tendencies. But now she saw him objectively and often felt relieved that she didn't have to put up with his inconsiderate behavior anymore.

Except that Nora often did, which inevitably made

Rebecca livid. Jack had never been a very consistent father, sometimes showering Nora with the attention and affection she deserved and sometimes ignoring her existence completely. His sales job kept him on the road a lot, and even when he was in town, he often forgot plans and special dates he'd made with Nora. Rebecca was left to make excuses and soothe Nora's hurt feelings…and to give their daughter a double share of love and attention. It was at those times especially that Rebecca wondered why she'd ever put up with him all those years.

Rebecca had swiftly regained her pride in the years since her divorce, yet she'd never found the courage to have a real relationship again. She'd dated a bit, even met a few men she genuinely liked. But nothing ever went too far, and Rebecca knew that the fault was hers alone. She never let her fledgling relationships progress very far and always found some reason to bail out before things grew serious.

It was fear, plain and simple. She didn't need a therapist or self-help guru to diagnose her problem. Logically she knew all men weren't faithless, but emotionally, she just didn't trust the opposite sex any longer. Besides, she'd found that earning a living and taking care of Nora required her full attention and effort. Though she was occasionally lonely and from time to time imagined a perfect romance that could magically sweep away her fears, Rebecca was largely content with her life and always put off the idea of dating for some future time in her life.

When Nora was older, she told herself, or when her professional life was less demanding of her time and energy. She knew these reasons were all thin excuses, convenient shields. But she allowed herself the pretense and fended off friends and relations—mostly her two sisters—who never grew tired of trying to fix her up with dates.

At least by living at the Berringers' for the summer she'd be out of that loop, Rebecca reflected, and the relative isolation would give her the perfect excuse to neglect her love life, or lack thereof.

The week passed quickly and the morning soon arrived for Rebecca and Nora to drive to Bridge-hampton in Rebecca's aged and overloaded car. She'd hired two college students with a van to move her furniture and many of the boxes.

All in all, she didn't have much to show in the way of worldly goods, which was more or less the way she preferred it. Rebecca had never been impressed by wealth or the privilege and power it commanded. Her ex-husband had often accused her of what he called reverse snobbery, and though she was sure she wasn't usually judgmental, she sometimes thought she did have an automatic bias against rich people. Matthew Berringer, however, had impressed her favorably, and for all his money, she had found him quite down-to-earth. As for her new patient, Rebecca thought as she turned down the long drive that led to the mansion, well…any snobbery Grant Berringer possessed was the least of her problems right now.

"Wow…we're going to live in *there?*" Nora asked with a gasp.

Rebecca had to laugh at her reaction. "That's right."

"It does look like a castle...practically," Nora conceded.

"It's as close as we'll ever get, honey," Rebecca replied. As if to underscore her advice, Eloise, in her cat carrier, released a long, plaintive yowl.

As soon as Rebecca and Nora arrived, Matthew sent down some of the house staff to help, and the car and van were unpacked in no time flat. Rebecca felt a bit disoriented by the moving-day confusion, especially since Nora insisted on opening various boxes, looking for favorite toys and other belongings she feared Rebecca had left behind. Rebecca had hoped to put their things away in an orderly fashion, but soon the place was topsy-turvy.

In the midst of the confusion, the phone rang, and Rebecca was greeted by Grant's deep, commanding voice.

"So, you've finally arrived. When did you plan on seeing your patient...next week, perhaps?" he asked in a cranky tone.

For a man who had to be persuaded to hire her, he was certainly taking a different tack today, she reflected. Different, but no less imperious.

"I was just doing a bit of unpacking. Do you feel neglected already?" she countered.

She was probably starting off on the entirely wrong foot—and would be fired by dinnertime, hence wasting energy with all the effort of moving in—but he sounded so much like a spoiled little boy, she couldn't resist answering him tartly.

"That's not the point." He bristled. "I believe that you're to be paid very well for your time here, Ms.

Calloway, and I expect your complete attention. Is that clear?''

"Quite clear. Though, in fact, you don't start paying me for my time until Monday morning, and today is Saturday,'' she reminded him politely. "Also, please feel free to call me Rebecca.''

She heard him grumble but couldn't make out the words. She didn't expect an apology, and there was none.

She did expect him to hang up, but instead he said, "It's almost twelve o'clock. If you haven't had any lunch yet, please join me. On the terrace off the library, in about half an hour or so.''

It was more of a command than an invitation, Rebecca noticed, but it seemed to indicate that he was eager to see her again, which was a hopeful sign.

"Thank you, I'll see you then.'' She hung up the phone, checked her watch and quickly glanced at herself and then Nora. They both looked as if they'd been dragged through a trashbin by the hair. They'd never be ready on time, but Rebecca knew she had better try.

Miraculously, a half hour later, she had bathed Nora, dressed her in a yellow gingham sundress and sandals and put her long hair in a ponytail. No time for a braid. Nora didn't understand why she had to suddenly dress up but submitted to the treatment with little complaint. Rebecca had quickly showered, pulled on a long floral skirt and silk tank top she'd found at the top of the clothes pile and then whisked on some lipstick. She grabbed Nora's hand, and they scurried down numerous hallways until they finally found the library. Nora thought it was a game and raced ahead, despite Rebecca's hushed warnings to slow down.

A bit out of breath but right on time, Rebecca composed herself at the door to the library. She took a deep breath and smoothed her hair before entering. The room was empty, but she heard voices outside the glass doors that opened to the terrace. As she stepped onto the terrace, she saw Matthew and Grant sitting at a table set for lunch. Rebecca stopped a few feet away from the table and smiled at them both.

"Well, here we are," she said brightly.

"And right on time," Matthew replied with a smile. He rose to greet them. "How nice to be joined for lunch by two lovely ladies."

Rebecca smiled in reply as he held out her chair. But when she turned to greet Grant, his dark gaze was narrowed, his brow knitted in a frown. He stared at her, looking positively shocked. She couldn't quite figure it out. Then she realized he was staring at Nora.

"Who's that?" he demanded, indicating Nora.

Rebecca felt her daughter clutch her hand and looked to see the child's expression grow wary and tense. She pulled her protectively to her side. "My daughter. Her name is Nora."

"You never said you were bringing a child," he bellowed.

Rebecca glanced nervously from Grant to Matthew, who seemed to shrink into his seat. "But…I told Matthew. I assumed he told you," she explained.

Grant's dark eyes widened, and his mouth tightened into a hard, grim line. He stared across the table at his brother. "You knew she was bringing a child here?" he demanded.

"Rebecca told me about her daughter during her interview," Matthew admitted smoothly. "We'll discuss this later, Grant. No reason to frighten the little girl."

"No reason, eh? No reason to tell me about the child, either, I suppose...until it's too late. Because you knew I wouldn't permit it!" he roared. His fiery gaze swept from Matthew to Rebecca. "And I won't," he insisted.

Rebecca took a deep breath and stood tall against his outburst. She didn't know what to say. If Matthew knew his brother had such strong objections to having a child in the house and had hidden Nora's arrival from Grant, then she could understand Grant's anger. Not that it excused his manner of expressing it.

"Grant, please." Matthew approached his brother. "Calm down. Try to be more reasonable—"

"Why in heaven's name should I be reasonable? You've purposely tricked me. The both of you. Just because I'm in a wheelchair, does that mean you have a right to control and manipulate me? To completely ignore my opinion?" He backed his wheelchair away from the table, then came directly toward Rebecca and Nora.

His dark hair looked longer and shaggier than at their first meeting, Rebecca thought. And his glowing lion's eyes burned bright and wild. Even in his anger, Rebecca still felt that irksome tug of attraction she tried so hard to deny.

He was acting like a child, she told herself. Still,

she understood his side of the situation. He was a proud man, now forced to rely on others for every need. It was a question of self-respect. She was sorry she had not been aware of his objection. She would have confronted him directly about it, as an equal. Now he seemed to believe she was in on the deception.

"I wasn't aware that you didn't want to hire someone with a child," she said honestly. "It's a big house. Nora will do her best to stay out of your way. If that's not a satisfactory solution, we can go."

He rolled the chair closer, glaring at her. "I would like you to go," he announced in a low, harsh tone. "Today, if at all possible."

"Grant—come on now," Matthew urged. "Rebecca has a contract."

"What's the difference? Pay her out. Pay her for the whole damn summer. What do I care?"

"But why must she go?" Matthew persisted. "It was all my fault. You can't just—"

"Don't tell me what I can and cannot do!" Grant turned toward his brother and pounded his fist on the tabletop. The plates and silverware clattered. "I'll do as I damn please! Do you understand that?"

Clinging to Rebecca's side, Nora suddenly burst into tears and buried her face in her mother's skirt. Rebecca was overwhelmed by a wave of protective instinct.

"Nora, sweetheart," she crooned. "It's okay." She crouched and wrapped her arms around the little girl in a sheltering embrace.

"Can't we go, Mommy? He's...scaring me," Nora whispered between sniffles.

"Don't be afraid, sweetie. We're going right away," she promised.

She scooped Nora up in her arms, though the child was well past the age of easy lifting. Nora clung to her and buried her face in her mother's shoulder. If this was the atmosphere Grant would create, then perhaps it was best if she took Nora away. As she turned to leave the terrace, Rebecca glanced at Grant with a searing look.

"Proud of yourself?" she asked, though she didn't know how she dared to be so insolent to him.

The look he gave her in answer stopped her cold in her tracks. His eyes flashed, and he looked away, quickly turning his chair so he didn't have to face her.

"You don't have a clue about me, Rebecca Calloway," he said in a hushed, almost apologetic tone. "It's best you get away now, while the going is good. Best for your little girl, too."

Rebecca stood stone still for a moment, feeling dazed and confused. But before she could think of anything to say in reply, Grant turned his chair, and she was suddenly facing his back. Matthew glanced at her and made a small motion with his head, indicating that she should leave them.

Hugging Nora close, she made her way through the study and down the labyrinth of hallways to their rooms. Nora had calmed down considerably and didn't need to be carried all the way—which Rebecca considered a small blessing, since her back was al-

ready sore from moving, and she faced repacking
many boxes and loading her car again.

Once in their rooms, Rebecca explained that Grant
was not a bad person and that his outburst didn't have
anything to do with Nora personally. She told her
daughter he was terribly unhappy because of his accident and slow recovery. Nora seemed to understand.

A few minutes later, Matthew brought them some
lunch on a tray. Nora immediately ran over and chose
a sandwich. Rebecca had lost her appetite and picked
up a cold drink. Matthew moved a few boxes to the
floor, then sat on the small sofa and sighed.

"I need to apologize," he began. "This whole
mess is all my fault. I knew Grant would object to
having your daughter here, but I'd hoped that once
you arrived, he'd get used to the idea," he explained.

"What does he have against children?" she asked.
"Does he think having Nora with me will distract me
from my work?"

"No, it's not that." Matthew met her gaze then
looked away. "I'm not free to say. But maybe you
can talk to him about it. He might explain it to you."

"Why bother?" Rebecca asked honestly. "I doubt
he'll change his mind."

"Won't you stay? At least until Monday. Maybe
by then I can persuade him to reconsider."

Rebecca's first impulse was to say no. She found
the start an ill omen and had the instinct to bail out.
Something told her this job would be jinxed. Perhaps
it was best to get out now, before she'd begun. As
for her contract, she'd never accept the full summer's
salary for work she did not perform, as Grant had

suggested. But she did feel that the Berringers owed her expenses for her trouble in getting here and moving out.

Still, Rebecca knew she couldn't answer abruptly. Her professionalism demanded a rational pace. And though she hardly knew Matthew Berringer, she was beginning to feel as if they were friends. She couldn't just run out on him. Again, she wondered why she felt no attraction to Matthew, with his calm, considerate manner and even temperament. The two brothers were opposite in every way. It was just her luck that only the brooding, titanic Grant drew her.

"I don't know," she said finally. She crossed her arms over her chest. "Grant feels very strongly about the issue. And I do understand why he's angry."

Matthew dragged his hand through his hair. "Yes, yes. I know you're right. I made a big blunder there. It was wrong of me to hide the truth from him. I can see that now," he admitted. "But you only just got here. You can't turn around and go. Won't you stay the night? You and Nora must be exhausted. Grant isn't such a monster that he won't understand."

Rebecca shrugged. She glanced at the boxes. She had to laugh or she would cry.

The truth was, she had no place to go with Nora. They'd probably end up at a motel somewhere for the night, and maybe even until she could rent a new apartment. She might make the long drive to Connecticut and stay with her mother. But that wouldn't solve everything. Her head spun.

"Mommy!" Nora raced in from the other room, wild-eyed. She ran straight to Rebecca and clutched her arm. "Mommy, something horrible has happened," she gasped, on the verge of tears.

Rebecca gripped her shoulders and remained calm. Sometimes Nora's emergencies were nothing more than a lost button or a bit of chocolate candy melted in a coat pocket.

"What is it, Nora? What's happened?"

"Eloise," she gasped. "She's gone. I wanted to feed her some of my sandwich and I looked everywhere. She must have run away."

Rebecca felt her stomach clench but tried to be reasonable. "She must be around here somewhere, sweetheart. She's probably scared from the move and hiding in one of the boxes."

Nora shook her head. Tears welled in her eyes. "We only opened a few boxes and I checked them all. I've looked in the closets and under the bed. Everywhere," she insisted. "She's gone."

Rebecca hoped that was not the case. But a cold chill in her gut told her it was so. Nora was a smart girl, and if she said she had looked thoroughly, she had.

"What's happened?" Matthew asked quietly. "Did she lose something?"

Rebecca nodded. "Our cat. Seems she's disappeared."

"What a day." Matthew sighed and shook his head. "Well, I'm sure we'll find her. Though the cat could be anywhere in the house by now if she's wandered outside these rooms."

And it was a large house, Rebecca reflected grimly. A very large house.

"We've kept the door closed since we got here. But I guess she could have slipped out when we weren't looking."

"No," Nora insisted. "She was sleeping under the bed when we left. But look." She pointed to a sliding glass door that opened to a deck. "That door was open. She could have gone out onto the beach and run away."

Rebecca looked at the door then at her daughter. It seemed to be the only explanation. She rested her hand on Nora's soft hair. "We'll go out and look right now. She's such a lazy old thing," Rebecca added. "She probably didn't get very far at all."

"Okay." Nora nodded. "Let's go." Rebecca could tell she was trying to be brave but was imagining the worst.

As Rebecca and Nora started toward the door to the deck, Matthew picked up the phone. "We'll get some help from the household staff. We'll make a complete search of the house and grounds. Don't worry, Nora. We'll find your cat," he promised.

Nora thanked him, and her eyes brightened. Rebecca was grateful for the help.

Three

With the help of several members of the Berringer household staff, including the housekeeper, Mrs. Walker and Matthew, they searched for hours—the house, the grounds and the beach. They searched the large garage, the pool side cabana, the guest cottage and gardener's shed without a sign or fleeting sighting of Eloise.

It was dark by the time Rebecca convinced Nora to give up and return to their apartment. The little girl was too exhausted to argue and too tired to eat any supper. Rebecca washed her quickly and pulled on her nightgown.

''Don't worry, we'll look again tomorrow morning,'' Rebecca promised her as she tucked Nora in. ''She couldn't have simply disappeared.''

''Oh, yes, she could,'' Nora murmured sadly.

"Don't you remember the cat in Alice in Wonderland? The Cheddar cat?"

"The Cheddar cat?" Then Rebecca realized she meant the Cheshire cat. But before she could reply, Nora had turned her tearstained face into her pillow and fallen asleep.

Rebecca felt bone tired, and after a quick shower, she climbed into her bed and shut off the light. Losing a job, a cat and the roof over their heads all in one day had been draining, to say the least.

She wondered if Grant Berringer knew they had not yet left. Well, there was no hope for that. But tomorrow morning, with or without Eloise, they had to be on their way. Tomorrow had to be a better day, she reflected as she drifted off to sleep. What else could possibly go wrong?

Rebecca was awakened by the shrill sound of the telephone. Early morning light filtered through the drawn curtains. She glanced at the clock on the nightstand. It was barely seven, and she wondered who could be calling so early.

It was Grant. He greeted her in his deep, sonorous tone, which danced along her nerve endings like an electric charge. Rebecca was annoyed at herself for feeling the least bit affected by him.

"If you're checking to see if we've left yet, don't worry," she said curtly. "We'll be gone in an hour or so."

"Well, don't forget your cat," he replied in a voice that could almost be called cheerful. "A large calico, on the plump side? The tag says her name is Eloise."

Rebecca quickly sat up. "How did you find Eloise?"

"She found me. When I woke this morning, she was sleeping at the foot of my bed. She's now helping herself to my breakfast. She's enjoying the cream cheese and lox but doesn't have much interest in the bagel."

As if Grant wasn't mad enough at them already, now the cat was prancing through his breakfast. She decided she ought to get over there in a hurry, before he lost his temper and frightened Eloise back into oblivion.

"I'll be there right away. Try to hold on to her."

"I don't think she's going anywhere," he replied, clearly amused at her urgency. "Not as long as the smoked salmon holds out."

Rebecca ended the conversation abruptly and jumped out of bed. As she frantically searched through a box of clothes for her bathrobe, Nora woke up and came into her room.

"What's the matter? Who was that on the phone, Mommy?"

"Mr. Berringer found Eloise. I'm going to get her."

Nora beamed and jumped with excitement. "I want to come get her...please?"

Rebecca pulled on her robe and tied the sash. "You wait here, honey. It's better if I go alone. I'll be right back."

"Please? Why can't I come, too?" Nora pleaded. "Matthew won't mind if I come with you."

"It wasn't Matthew who called. It was Grant," Rebecca explained. Suddenly, Nora did not seem as eager to come.

"Oh. Was he angry?" she asked.

"He didn't sound angry," Rebecca answered honestly. "Not at all. He's feeding Eloise breakfast. I'm sure she's safe and sound."

"All right. But come right back." Nora made her promise. Then she ran into her room and returned with the cat carrier. "And be sure to put her in here right away, so she doesn't run away again."

"Good thinking." Rebecca took the carrier and left on her mission.

It wasn't until she knocked on Grant's door that she suddenly gave a thought to her appearance. She hadn't bothered to comb her hair, which hung in loose, long reddish brown waves past her shoulders. She'd pulled on the first nightgown she'd found last night, a short slip style in shell pink, and a handy robe—a peach-colored floral print that ended mid-thigh. She suddenly felt exposed and vulnerable, and at a distinct disadvantage, facing him again wearing such flimsy attire. But there was no help for it now.

"Come in," he replied from the other side of the door.

Rebecca opened the door slowly and spotted Grant, sitting near the doors that led to the deck. The curtains had been pulled back and the room was filled with soft morning light. As she entered, she held the cat carrier in front of her, hoping it would distract him from her scanty attire and long, bare legs.

She didn't see the cat anywhere and wondered if she had gotten away again. Then she realized Eloise was sitting in Grant's lap, curled in a comfortable ball and cleaning her face with one paw.

"Oh, dear. I'm sorry," Rebecca apologized, quickly walking toward him. "Let me get her off you."

"It's all right." Grant held up his hand. "She's not bothering me…and I did want to speak to you."

"Oh. About what?" Rebecca took a step closer and held the cat carrier at her side. She felt self-conscious as Grant paused, seeming to forget what he wanted to talk about.

His dark, assessing gaze moved over her from the top of her head to her bare feet. When their gazes met again, the smoldering light in his eyes was one of pure male appreciation—and more than that, desire.

"You came straight from your bed, I see," he commented finally. His voice was low and husky, and she was sure that wasn't at all what he'd meant to say.

She swallowed hard, feeling a hot blush sweep up her neck to color her cheeks as her body responded to his lustful look. She struggled to ignore the frisson of heat arcing between them and forced herself to sound businesslike and impersonal.

"You wanted to speak to me about something?" she reminded him.

He looked away and shifted in his chair. "I wanted to apologize for my outburst yesterday. I'm ashamed of myself. Totally. And very sorry for frightening your daughter. Will you tell her that I'm sorry and didn't mean to scare her?"

She was surprised, not just by his words, but his sincere, heartfelt tone. "Thank you for saying that.

Yes, I'll give Nora your apology," she promised. "I'm sure she's already forgiven you since you found the cat."

"And what about you, Rebecca? Do you forgive me?"

Rebecca took a breath. "I do…though I can't see why it should matter," she answered honestly. "After today, we'll probably never see each other again."

She knew the words were true, yet somehow the thought of never seeing him again seemed impossible. Unthinkable, actually. She felt a powerful, uncanny connection to him. The intimacy caused by the fact that they were both in their pajamas, just out of bed, somehow didn't seem strange at all.

"Would you consider staying? I know it's a lot to ask after the way I acted." He shook his head. "There is a reason for my reaction. Though it's still no excuse."

"Oh? And what's that?"

He seemed to be collecting his thoughts. A lock of his dark hair fell across his forehead, and he brushed it back. He hadn't shaved yet, and a day's growth of beard shadowed his lean cheeks. He wore long striped pajama bottoms. Either he'd been in excellent shape before the accident, or using the wheelchair for weeks had built up his shoulders, chest and arms. His dark blue silk robe hung open, exposing his muscular, hair-covered chest, completing an image that was thoroughly masculine and totally appealing. Rebecca realized she was staring and forced herself to look away.

"My fiancée, Courtney…she was expecting our

baby when she died. Now I find it hard to be around children.'' Rebecca felt her breath catch in her throat at his admission. Poor man. If there was an acceptable excuse for his outburst, this had to be it.

''I'm so sorry...I had no idea,'' Rebecca replied. She didn't know what more to say. She watched as he took a deep breath, struggling to maintain control.

''Of course you didn't,'' he replied. ''But the world is full of children, and I can't hide from that fact forever.'' He paused again. ''Yesterday, after you ran off with Nora, I had to face myself—my own selfishness and insensitivity. The sight was repellent to me. I have to do better.''

He met her gaze for an instant, then looked away. His face was as devoid of emotion as his calm, even voice. But in his eyes Rebecca discovered a world of anguish and remorse.

She didn't know what to say, how to answer him. She sat on the edge of his bed next to the wheelchair. Her bare leg brushed the cool, smooth fabric of his robe. She had the urge to take his hand, to offer some gesture of physical comfort, but didn't quite dare.

''If you'll stay, I'll treat your daughter with kindness and respect,'' he promised. ''And the cat, too, of course,'' he added, stroking the contented feline who sat with eyes half-closed, like a furred Buddha in his lap.

''Yes, we'll stay,'' she replied in a quiet but firm tone. She had no need to think the matter over. But she knew she had to change the mood, to snap him out of this reverie and get him looking to the future.

''The clock starts running officially tomorrow.

We'll start very early in the morning, too. I'm going to put you to work," she warned him. "Hard work."

"Oh, hard work, eh? You sound as if you think I've had it easy so far, Rebecca. Lolling about, reading girlie magazines or something?" The grief that had shadowed his handsome features had faded. A sexy, winsome smile played at the corners of his full lips and set her pulse on an erratic pace.

"I won't comment on your taste in literature. But you asked me to get you out of that wheelchair by the end of summer, and I mean to do it."

"Yes, sir!" He teased her with a curt salute. Alarmed at the gesture, Eloise jumped off Grant's lap and strolled to an armchair, where she jumped up and settled.

"Okay, laugh if you like." Her take-charge tone had amused him. That was fine for now. He wouldn't be quite so amused come tomorrow, she reflected with a secret smile.

"I'm not laughing at you...but you do make me smile a lot," he admitted. He regarded her with a thoughtful expression. "Maybe that's the reason I hired you, after all."

"Maybe," she replied, her gaze still locked on his.

His dark gaze made her feel warm. She wanted to look away but couldn't and watched, mesmerized, as his gaze wandered over her face, studying her—liking what he saw, it seemed—finally dropping to her lips.

"You know, you're very lovely. Beautiful, really," he said. "Not many women could sit in the full morning light without a drop of makeup on looking as lovely as you do."

Compliments about her physical appearance always made Rebecca uncomfortable, mostly because she could never quite believe them. She felt herself flush with embarrassment. He sounded as if he knew what he was talking about when it came to women, and she imagined he'd seen more than his fair share of females first thing in the morning. The thought was a sobering one.

"Did you hire me for my good looks?" she asked curtly. "I thought it was for my brains."

"To be honest, I hardly noticed what you looked like when you came for the interview." The statement stung, but Rebecca knew he was being truthful. "Now that I have, let's just say that if I'm going to be saddled with a tyrant all summer, she may as well be easy on the eyes." He gave her a tigerlike grin. "And blush so prettily when I tease her."

She opened her mouth to protest, but before she could utter a sound, he reached out and cupped her cheek with his hand. He was about to kiss her, and her breath caught in her throat. He couldn't kiss her, her mind protested. This moment between them had gone way out of control.

But somehow, she couldn't move away. As his large hand stroked her cheek and the pad of his thumb swept over her full bottom lip, instead of moving away, she leaned closer, so close she felt the heat of his breath on her skin. When his long fingers sifted her hair, urging her closer, she rested her hand on his forearm and felt his formidable strength.

"Grant…this is not a good way to start things off," she finally whispered.

''We don't start officially until tomorrow morning. You just said so yourself,'' he reminded her, his lips barely a breath away from hers.

''But I didn't mean...'' Her halfhearted protest was abruptly interrupted as his mouth covered hers. His lips were warm, his touch coaxing and persuasive.

Though she wanted to pull away for a moment, struggling to resist, the sensation of his mouth on hers quickly melted her defenses. There was nothing tentative in his kiss. Not in the least. His lips moved over hers masterfully, savoring her response and persuading her to give him more and more. His strong arms wrapped around her, and his tongue slipped into her mouth, and she heard herself give a small moan of pleasure, a sound that encouraged him even more.

She knew she had to stop him...but she couldn't stop herself. All her hesitation and doubts about taking this job boiled down to one thing—her compelling attraction to him. A powerful pull that was all the more dangerous because he seemed to share the feeling.

Their attraction had simmered below the surface since they'd met—and now, sitting here in such an intimate atmosphere, it had exploded.

Rebecca couldn't reason, couldn't protest. She couldn't stop kissing him or resist the mounting pleasure of him kissing her. Their intense attraction had somehow moved them to another place, and the moment seemed separate from the real world. Pure and elemental. She wasn't his therapist, only a woman expressing her longing, and he was not her patient, but a passionate man who desired her totally.

She leaned her head back and felt him clutch her shoulders. Her mouth opened under his, and the kiss deepened, rising in intensity and hunger. She pressed her hand to his chest. At the opening of his robe, she felt the whorls of dark hair and warm skin. Instinctively, her fingers glided across his chest in a smooth caress.

She heard him moan deep in his throat, and the sound excited her. His strong hands pushed her robe down her arms, then slid down her bare arms, leaving a fiery path in their wake. Then she felt his caressing touch on her breasts, the heat of his hands penetrating the thin silky fabric of her nightgown. Her nipples grew instantly tight and tingled as he stroked them with his fingertips. She pulled her mouth from his, and her head dropped to his shoulder. She covered his hands with hers and stilled them. She felt too weak to pull away from him, but knew it could go no further. She was shocked and amazed it had gone this far.

"We have to stop. Please," she whispered.

He pressed his cheek to her hair and didn't say anything at first. She wondered if he had heard her. Finally, she lifted her head and stared into his eyes.

"Yes, you're right." He nodded.

He looked at her body and then gently pulled up her robe. The lightest touch of his fingertips on her skin set her nerves jumping with excitement. She pulled away from him and struggled to ignore the sensation.

"We're attracted to each other. It happens," she said, trying to regain some control.

"Oh…does this happen *often* to you? With your patients, I mean?" he asked, eyes wide, dark brows raised.

"Of course not!" she exclaimed. "It's never happened…I've never so much as… Well, I've certainly never kissed a patient before," she insisted.

"I've never kissed a therapist, so I suppose we're even."

He didn't sound as if he believed her, and though the thought made her angry, she couldn't entirely blame him. She'd behaved like a love-starved loon. What did he think she was, a paid companion? How was she ever going to set things right here?

"Look, what I meant to say was, it shouldn't have happened. But it did. We're attracted to each other… and curious, I suppose," she reasoned. "Maybe it's a good thing it happened now, and we've gotten it out and over with."

"You sound as if kissing me was some distasteful but necessary task, Rebecca." He sounded stung. Rebecca nearly laughed.

"I didn't say I didn't enjoy it," she argued. "But it was totally…inappropriate."

"Inappropriate, yes. The best ones usually are."

His smug, sexy grin was infuriating. She had enjoyed it. More than he could know or she'd ever be willing to admit. But it wouldn't happen again.

She stood up and pushed her hair from her face. He'd gotten her so confused, her head was spinning.

"Look, let's get the ground rules straight right now." She commanded his attention with her best professional manner. "As the weeks pass, we will have a close relationship. Even a physical relationship. But *not* a romantic one. This cannot happen again. Or I'm out of here. Contract or not. Understand?''

''Yes.'' He nodded. ''I understand completely.''

She thought for a moment he might apologize. But he didn't. Although his face held a completely serious expression, in his eyes she could still detect a gleam of male satisfaction. As if they'd been playing some game and he'd won the first round, hands down.

Of course, it had all been a game to him.

An amusement for a man who was by now probably bored with his own company. He couldn't really be attracted to her, she reasoned. Not seriously, anyway. She suspected that he was still too much in love with his fiancée, for one thing.

He was testing her. And testing his ability to attract and relate to women again. It was important to remember that, she realized.

From that perspective, it was probably a good sign that he'd made some move toward her. It was all part of his recovery process, and she felt a great deal better about the encounter thinking of it in those terms.

The awkward moment was cut short by a sharp knock on the door. Rebecca quickly put some distance between herself and Grant. She checked her robe to make sure it was securely fastened. Even if it was one of the housekeeping staff, coming to clear away his breakfast tray, she thought it looked awfully questionable to be found in her nightgown and robe in Grant's room so early in the morning.

''Come in,'' Grant called.

The door opened slowly, and Nora peeked from behind it.

Rebecca could see in a glance that her yearning to see Eloise had overruled her fear of disobeying her mother and facing Grant, the monster.

"Nora. Did you follow me? I asked you to wait in our rooms," Rebecca reminded her calmly. Secretly, she was most grateful that Nora had not interrupted them a few moments earlier.

"But I waited and waited and you never came back. Did Eloise get lost again?"

"Don't worry. She's safe and sound," Grant assured her. He wheeled his chair toward Nora.

"Where is she?" Nora asked, glancing around the room. "I don't see her."

"Right there, on the chair." Grant pointed to Eloise. "She ate a hearty breakfast and needed a nap."

Nora leaned around the door and saw the cat. But Rebecca could tell she was still afraid of getting too close to Grant.

"Come in, come in," he urged her. "I won't bite you."

"You won't?" Nora asked doubtfully. Her abrupt reply made the adults laugh.

"I deserve that," Grant said, shaking his head. Rebecca could see genuine regret in his dark eyes, and his caring spirit touched her. "I'm sorry I scared you, Nora. Very sorry. I'm not usually like that. It was wrong of me. I won't do it again," he promised. "I've just got a bad temper, being in this chair," he explained, slapping the side of the chair with his hand.

"Mommy said you got hurt in a car accident and sometimes when people take a long time to get better, they feel angry. She said it didn't have anything to do with me," Nora explained.

Grant glanced from Nora to Rebecca. Their gazes met for an instant, and his look was a mixture of embarrassment at being read so clearly and respect for Rebecca's insight.

"Your mother is a very smart woman."

"Yes, I know," Nora replied in a matter-of-fact tone.

"I've asked her to stay here and help me get better. Is that okay with you?"

Nora took a moment to appraise him with intelligent eyes. Rebecca felt quite proud of her. "It's okay. She has to do her work." She finally stepped into the room. "Thank you for finding Eloise, Mr. Berringer."

She walked to the armchair to get her cat and Grant's gaze followed her. "You call me Grant," he told her. "And actually, your cat, found me. By the way, I was wondering, how did she get that name, Eloise?" he asked with genuine curiosity.

"I named her after the character in the books. You know, the little girl who lives in the Plaza Hotel in New York City." Nora sat next to her cat and began to pet her. The cat lifted her head and pressed against Nora's hand, then rose and jumped into Nora's arms. "She's very rich and spoiled and orders anything she wants from room service, and does whatever she likes and never has to pay attention to grown-ups."

"She sounds...charming," Grant remarked with a sly smile, and Rebecca found herself smiling, too.

"I'd like to read about her sometime. Maybe you could loan that book to me."

"Maybe. Or I could read it to you," Nora suggested. "I can read, you know."

"Can you really?" he replied, sounding suitably impressed. "Well, I'd like that very much."

His warm, delighted laugh transformed his features completely. His dark eyes flashed, and Rebecca felt her heartbeat quicken. She forced herself to look away.

"Have you ever been to the Plaza Hotel, Nora?" he asked.

Nora shook her head. "Mommy says she'll take me there when I'm a little older. Maybe for my next birthday. There's a portrait of Eloise there, you know. Right in the lobby."

"Is there? I've never noticed. You must see it then. I'll take you there myself. To make up for yesterday. How does that sound?"

Nora's eyes widened. "Would you really? That sounds great."

Rebecca could tell from Nora's expression that all was forgiven. She felt pleased and proud of both of them. Nora had been brave to face Grant and work out her problem with him without her mother's help, Rebecca thought. And as for Grant, Rebecca felt heartened to see she had not been so far off in her impression of him as a kind, sensitive man—despite the way he'd behaved yesterday. It was obvious he wasn't around children much, but still, he had a nice way of relating to Nora, she thought.

Promising to take Nora to the Plaza was a grand

gesture, but would he really carry through on it? Rebecca wondered. Perhaps he didn't realize Nora would not easily forget the idea. Oh, well, she'd manage to make it up to Nora once they got back to the city. She was happy to see that Grant could treat Nora kindly and that Nora had gotten over her initial fear of him. This newly forged truce between the two would certainly make her work easier.

Now if only she could negotiate a truce in her own heart with her seesawing feelings of attraction for him.

Four

"Seventeen, eighteen…come on, lazy bones," Rebecca chided him. "You're not getting off this bench until you give me thirty good ones."

"Twenty-five…and I'll raise your salary." He huffed as he completed two more lifts.

"You can't buy yourself out of this torture," she teased. "Besides, I thought you knew by now I can't be bribed. Twenty-one… That's good, nine more."

"Nine more! Ugh," he groaned, completing another lift. "You're a slave driver…a cruel, heartless wench. It's hard to believe it, looking at you…" He huffed.

"No pain, no gain, pal."

"You sadists all love that line, don't you?" Grant grunted.

"Do save your breath for the exercises, Grant,"

she counseled him. "You still haven't hit the bench press today."

She watched the muscles in his thighs bunch and his jaw clench as he pushed himself to reach number thirty. He was making an effort, a painful one. Pleased with his physical progress and spirit, she didn't care a whit what he called her.

"The bench press!" He railed between breaths. "What are you trying to turn me into, woman? I work on Wall Street, remember? Not as a bouncer in a nightclub."

Rebecca had to laugh. "True, but a little bulk under your Armani suits couldn't hurt. You still need to intimidate the other guy when you swing those big deals, don't you?"

"I intimidate them with my intelligence, daring and reputation as a financial piranha, not with my neck size." He gasped.

"Breathe," she reminded. "In through the mouth, leg up, out through the nose, leg down. Slowly now. I want concentration and control."

His nostrils flared as he exhaled a long breath. "Yes, master," he replied.

"That's the idea." She praised him with a laugh.

In a month's time, they had made impressive progress. As she had feared, Grant was resistant and hard to motivate at first. Yet during those early days, he never challenged her so seriously that she gave up on him and quit. Little by little, day by day, she watched his resistance slowly wear away and saw him become increasingly committed to his recuperation.

When she came to him in the mornings, he looked

pleased to see her and begin their workout—though he greeted her with every disparaging name in the book. But Rebecca knew he didn't really mean it. It was just his way of dealing with the fear of trying hard and maybe failing.

But he wasn't failing. Not in the least. He was succeeding by leaps and bounds. In a day or so, he'd be ready to leave his wheelchair and graduate to crutches. When Rebecca had reported the news to Matthew, she saw tears in his eyes. But he briskly brushed the emotional moment aside.

Although Matthew insisted she was indeed a miracle worker to get Grant interested in a therapy program, Rebecca knew it was not merely her coaching and praise that motivated him. She knew Grant was far more motivated and inspired each time he could see that he'd gained strength and some use of his injured body. Getting out of the wheelchair was a particularly enticing carrot to dangle in front of him. She knew the move would be a great boost to his spirits and his self-image. Once on his feet, even supported by crutches, he would start to see himself again as the vital, energetic and confident man he once had been.

Rebecca looked forward to the change with a mixture of pleasure and fear. It had been hard enough to handle her feelings of attraction toward him and keep their relationship within professional limits while he was wheelchair-bound. But as he grew stronger, her willpower seemed to grow weaker. She didn't know how she'd manage to hold up her defenses against him once he got his full strength back.

Though he'd never tried to kiss her or encourage a romantic embrace after that first time weeks ago, Rebecca could always feel the powerful chemistry simmering between them, like some highly potent, combustible element that needed merely a spark to explode. No matter what she did, no matter how ultraprofessional she tried to act, how poker-faced and detached, it was always just there. The way he held her gaze when she smiled. The way he looked at her when he thought she didn't notice. The way his breathing changed and his body grew taut, affected by her slightest touch.

It had been so very long since Rebecca felt this way about a man. It was all so confusing, so disturbing to her peace of mind, and yet at the same so amazing. So downright…wonderful.

But she knew she could never let herself get carried away by high-school-girl feelings. To encourage any type of romantic relationship with a patient was totally unethical, even predatory in a way. In relationships between patients and medical professionals of any kind, so many patients mistook gratitude for feelings of love when they were recovering. Grant had experienced a serious blow to his ego and needed reassurance that he was still attractive to the opposite sex—thus the reason for that mind-blowing kiss and all the lingering looks that had come after. Since she was the only woman in his life right now—with the exception of Mrs. Walker, who had to be in her mid-sixties—Grant's need to build up his macho confidence would have to be worked out with her.

It all sounded so simplistic, so obvious. She knew

if she ever tried to explain it to him, he'd laugh in her face and act as if he was above such predictable, textbook responses. But while Grant was a highly sophisticated man, he was no less vulnerable to his reactions and needs. Whatever he felt for her right now was a side effect of his recovery, Rebecca assured herself, and she would be foolish to take his admiration to heart.

Rebecca knew she, too, was especially vulnerable right now. Since Jack's betrayal, she hadn't been able to trust men. She certainly had let Grant closer emotionally than any man she'd met since her divorce. But was she attracted to him because his admiration was a great ego boost? Rebecca knew that was highly possible.

And what about Courtney? Was she his past love, or were Grant's feelings for her still very much in the present? Although he never spoke about his loss, he kept Courtney's photo at his bedside. She had been quite beautiful, with thick blond hair and a model's perfect features and figure. Rebecca had heard that Courtney had been a successful lawyer, as well.

Grant slept with Courtney's image just inches from his pillow. Rebecca could only imagine the tortured thoughts that ran through his head each night. Clearly he had never resolved his feelings of love for Courtney, and due to his memory loss, perhaps he never would.

Rebecca knew any woman with half a brain and an ounce of experience would be wary of losing her heart to a man who carried such a burden. Rebecca's heart went out to him, but the shadow of his past was

certainly one more good reason to avoid any real in-
volvement with Grant Berringer.

Turning her attention to the red-faced Grant, Rebecca realized he'd finally reached his goal.

"Thirty!" she announced brightly. He finished his
last leg lift and immediately collapsed onto the cush-
ion of the machinery with his eyes closed. "I knew
you could do it," she praised him. "Here, have some
water."

She handed him a water bottle and watched as he
tipped his head back and with eyes shut drank thirst-
ily. His thick hair was damp, and sweat ran freely
down his face and chest, causing his thin tank top and
shorts to cling to his body. He paused once, to take
a deep breath and stretch, his hard chest expanding
and his arm muscles pumping up.

Rebecca felt a knot of attraction and longing for
him tighten in the pit of her stomach. She took in a
sharp breath and turned to grab a towel from a nearby
chair.

"Here you go," she said lightly, while inside, she
felt anything but light. "How do you feel? How is
your leg?"

He had most severely injured his right leg, and the
last group of exercises was designed to strengthen
those muscles.

He shrugged and slung the towel around his neck.
"Okay, I guess. It feels a little tight today," he admitted.

He looked at his leg and flexed his foot. She saw
the corner of his mouth twitch and guessed he felt
some pain but wouldn't admit it.

''Get up on the table and let me have a look,'' she said with concern.

She thought he was going to argue with her, but he submitted with a frown and a peeved look. With a little help from Rebecca, he maneuvered himself off the seat of the weight machine, moved to the padded massage table on crutches and hoisted himself to a sitting position, his long, muscular legs dangling over the edge of the table.

She ran her hand over the back of his bare leg. His skin felt damp, and the dark hair on his legs tickled her palm. She gently tested the tension in his calf muscles with her fingertips. They were knotted, and she wondered if she'd pushed him too hard. If he strained a muscle, they'd have a setback, which would affect not only his healing process but his spirits, as well. And his spirits had improved so much since she'd arrived.

''Does this hurt?'' she asked, gently massaging the muscle.

''No...it feels good, actually,'' he replied in a husky tone.

She massaged the muscle until she felt the knot dissolve. She moved her hand to the front of his leg, stroking from his ankle to his kneecap. Her hand finally came to rest at the hard quadriceps at the top of his thigh. She felt the muscle with her fingertips, tenderly testing for any knots or signs of overwork.

''How about this leg?'' she asked in a concerned, professional manner. With one hand still resting on his right thigh, she used her other hand to examine his left leg.

When her tenderly probing fingertips slipped beneath the edge of his workout shorts, she heard his quickly indrawn breath and saw him grip the arms of the chair. She looked at his face. From the tight expression, she couldn't tell if he was in pain or if her ministrations had elicited another, quite different response.

When her gaze met his, she realized in a flash what was happening. She felt a hot blush race up her neck and drew her hands off his legs as if she'd been touching stove burners.

But before she could move away, he reached out and grabbed her shoulders.

"You don't have to stop, Rebecca. I like the way you touch me," he murmured. His husky, seductive tone seemed to set every nerve ending in her body on fire. "I like it very much."

"Grant, please..." She tried to pull away, but he wouldn't let her. His arms and shoulders had become more powerful in the past weeks, and she knew she was no match against him. She felt trapped between his open legs. She tried to pull her gaze from his, but his shining black eyes commanded her full and complete attention.

"You know very well I wasn't touching you that way." She finally managed to speak. "I only needed to see if you have a cramped muscle."

He laughed low in his chest. "Well, I have one now, ma'am," he reported blithely. "But definitely not in my leg."

Rebecca didn't dare let her gaze drop below his waist. She already knew his claim to be true. He still held her arms, but his hold had loosened. He gently stroked her upper arms and shoulders.

She stared at him, her lips pursed in dismay, not realizing for one moment the tempting and provocative picture she presented to him. Wisps of reddish brown hair had come loose from her ponytail and curled around her face in long tendrils. Her fair skin—which never quite tanned—looked smooth and sun-kissed from her hours on the beach. Her white tank top and navy blue shorts showed off her figure to advantage, and she knew his steamy gaze roamed appreciatively over her full breasts and tight waist.

The way he looked her over made Rebecca's heartbeat race. It had been a long time since any man had showered her with such blatant appreciation. And Grant wasn't just any man. He was an extraordinary person, she'd come to see that. Not only because he was rich, a self-made millionaire and a brilliant success at his work. But for so many reasons…just because he was Grant.

As he stared at her hungrily, she felt herself softening under his touch, like a chocolate bar left in the sun. She felt herself leaning toward him, staring at his mouth, imagining what it would be like to kiss him again.…

But some rational part of her mind valiantly fought, and would not allow her to move one breath closer. Still, neither could she find the will to move away.

"Let go of me, Grant, please…" Her plea was a hushed whisper.

Grant shook his head. A small smile played at the edges of his mouth.

"No, I don't think so. I want you right where you are, Rebecca. In fact, I want you even closer," he decided, his voice low and compelling.

His large hand moved to cup her head, and an instant later, his mouth merged with hers in a kiss that was wild and hungry•and almost violent in its intensity.

Rebecca struggled against him, then finally gave herself over to the moment. She moaned under the hard pressure of his lips. Not in protest, but in answer to his passionate assault. She felt an explosion of sheer desire and longing for him. Grant groaned, too, and his kiss deepened, his tongue swirling and melding with hers, his large hands sliding seductively down her back to stroke and cup her bottom and pull her even closer against the warmth at the juncture of his thighs.

Rebecca sighed, kissing him with her whole heart, her whole being. Her senses were suddenly filled with him—the taste of him, the scent of his warm body, the feeling of his hard muscles and smooth skin. Her head spun, and her knees turned to water. She clung to his shoulders for support. She felt intoxicated and in over her head.

But more than that, as the embrace continued, she felt an amazing sense of completeness and utter calm, as if she were suddenly sitting in the eye of a storm. She felt a total and utter connection to this man— heart, mind and soul—that she'd never experienced before. Could this really happen to a person outside of a book or a movie? Her rational mind demanded to know. Could this be happening to her?

A sharp knock on the door brought them both to their senses. Rebecca pulled away, and Grant finally released her. He rubbed his face with both hands as Rebecca moved a safe, discreet distance away. With her back turned toward the door, she struggled to get her breathing under control.

The knock sounded again, more insistent this time. "Come in," Grant shouted.

"Hi, guys, I'm back. Need a hand with anything in here?" Joe greeted them.

If she hadn't felt so muddled and light-headed, Rebecca knew she would have laughed at Joe's innocent question. Instead, she stared at the male nurse as if he'd just dropped down from the moon. Joe sometimes helped with Grant's morning workout, but since Rebecca's arrival, his work hours had been reduced, and he usually arrived at the house around noon. She was half grateful for his early appearance, and half annoyed at it.

"We've just finished the exercises," Rebecca replied in as natural a voice as she could manage. "Grant has some muscle soreness, but the whirlpool should help. Why don't you help him change into his swimsuit and bring him to the pool?"

"But we never did our cooldown, Rebecca," Grant reminded her. "I hardly think it's fair that you work a guy into a lather and totally skip the cooldown." His reminder sounded innocent enough, but Rebecca knew when she was being baited.

She glanced at him just long enough to catch his taunting grin, then forced herself to look quickly away. She felt an annoying blush color her cheeks

and sensed Joe regarding them with a curious stare.
Somehow she maintained a placid expression.

"Just dump him in the pool, Joe. The deep end,"
she instructed calmly. "That ought to cool him off
fairly quickly."

And before either man could reply, she gathered
her belongings and left the room.

That night, Rebecca took Nora out to dinner in
town and then to a movie, a G-rated family comedy.
She was glad they had planned the evening out and
relieved that she was able to avoid Grant at dinner.
But while the movie flashed before her eyes, she
could barely concentrate. All she thought about was
Grant, picturing him eating his dinner alone in his
room, most likely wearing that brooding expression.
He can survive very well without us, Rebecca assured
herself, *with a house full of servants to do his bidding
besides.* Still, she felt she'd somehow snuck out and
left him flat.

Not that they ate with him every night. Some
nights, she fixed an easy supper for herself and Nora
in the bachelor kitchen in their suite. But most often,
they took dinner with Matthew and Grant in the large
dining room or on the terrace off the library.

Sometimes it was only the three of them, Rebecca,
Nora and Grant. Since Rebecca had arrived, Matthew
had returned to his responsibilities in the city and
stayed there during the week, returning to the seaside
mansion on the weekends. Rebecca missed his company. He was not only a friendly face and ally when
Grant grew surly, but he provided the perfect buffer—

and even convenient chaperon—for herself and her too-attractive patient.

Even with Nora at the table, Rebecca often felt a pull between herself and Grant that was almost too intense to be ignored—or resisted. Especially when dinner was over, after Nora had run off to get ready for bed and Rebecca remained, sipping coffee and chatting with Grant about nothing in particular. Considering how much time they spent together every day, it was amazing to her that they had so much to talk about. Sometimes they talked little, preferring to sit together and listen to the night sounds and admire the sight of the rising moon over the water.

The air was so clear compared to the city, Rebecca and Nora were amazed at the display of stars in the night sky. Grant seemed amused at first by their reaction, and Rebecca felt a bit self-conscious. Then one night, he surprised them with a huge, high-quality telescope, which one of the maids brought out with their dessert. Rebecca had little interest in learning the names of constellations. But she greatly enjoyed viewing the heavens, and she appreciated Grant's thoughtful gesture. She knew he didn't have to go out of his way to please her, and the fact that he had secretly thrilled and worried her.

After the movie, she and Nora stopped for ice cream, and Nora was eager to bring some back for Grant. She already knew his favorite flavor—Rocky Road—since they'd had a long, careful discussion on the topic. At first, Rebecca thought, why not? Then she discouraged the idea. She didn't need to be knocking on his door late at night, bearing gifts. He might misinterpret the gesture and assume she'd found an excuse to see him and continue the amorous episode from early in the day.

That was just the problem. She had to be very careful to avoid provocative situations. Or very soon she'd be in real trouble. Rebecca shook her head dolefully as she started the car and headed to the Berringer mansion.

The house was quiet and dark when they returned, and Nora went to sleep quickly. Rebecca, however, tossed and turned as sensual memories of Grant's embrace made it impossible for her to sleep. She finally got up to make herself a cup of herbal tea. But when she searched her cupboard, she realized she was out of tea. She slipped on her robe and headed to the kitchen, which seemed miles away through the dark house. She was about halfway there when she heard a low but distinct moaning sound. She realized she was near Grant's rooms and the sound was coming from within. She drew closer and kept very still, listening. The sound came again, louder. It sounded as if he was in real pain, and without giving propriety a thought, she opened his unlocked door and entered his bedroom.

The room was dimly lit with a night-light near the bed, and she could see the outline of his body laying flat, under the covers.

"Grant, it's me, Rebecca. What's wrong?" she called softly. Her first guess was that she had overworked his injured leg and that, as a result, he was experiencing severe leg cramps. But if so, he hadn't sat up to rub his legs, she noticed.

He moaned again, then screamed and moved his hands to his head. "No, no…let go. Damn it, let go," he called in an anguished tone.

Then she realized he was asleep. Asleep and having a nightmare. She knelt next to his bed and gently shook his shoulder. "Grant, wake up. You're dreaming. You're having a bad dream. Wake up now," she said.

He took her hand in a viselike grip, still asleep, she realized. "Oh, sweetheart…how could you?" His tone was bleak, tortured. Rebecca felt stunned.

"Grant." She spoke louder. She shook his hand. "It's me, Rebecca."

Suddenly he opened his eyes, shook his head as if to clear away the remnants of his nightmare, then lifted himself to a sitting position in the bed.

He stared at her, looking shocked. "Rebecca…I thought you were…" He paused and looked away. "Never mind," he mumbled.

She watched him rub his face with his hands. *You thought I was Courtney. Of course. Who else?* Rebecca knew she had no right to feel hurt, yet her heart stung at the realization.

"I was on the way to the kitchen for some tea and heard you moaning. I thought maybe you'd fallen down, or had a leg cramp."

"Yes, yes, of course." He nodded, though she wasn't sure her words had fully registered. His eyes still looked shadowed, dazed, as if he was somewhere between his frightening other realm and the real world.

She reached for the light on the bedside table, but

he stilled her hand. "No, don't put the light on," he said.

"All right." Rebecca complied. He did not let go of her hand. He held it securely in his, which rested on the sheet.

She heard him breathing hard, as if he'd just run a five-minute mile, and guessed that his heart was pounding, as well. Whatever he'd been dreaming of, it had been terrifying. She wasn't sure if she should ask him about it.

"Can I get you anything? A glass of water?" she offered. "A cup of tea?"

"No, thanks." He paused and took a deep breath. "Just stay a minute more, will you?" he asked quietly.

"If you like," she replied.

"Don't kneel on the floor like that. Sit up on the bed," he commanded her. He sat with his back resting against the wooden headboard and shifted to make room for her.

Rebecca hesitated. Being on a bed with Grant—no matter how stressed he seemed—was not a good idea. Now that her eyes had gotten used to the dark, she could see him clearly. Too clearly, she thought. He was wearing a form-fitting T-shirt with a deep V-shaped neckline that emphasized his broad shoulders and muscular, hair-covered chest. He smelled of bath soap and a spicy cologne, all mingled with another scent that was distinctly his alone. Distinctly male.

Then she chided herself for being silly. The man was practically traumatized from a nightmare. He was hardly in the mental state to be planning a seduction.

She sat on the edge of the bed with Grant still holding her hand. He was quiet for a long time. Rebecca heard his breathing return to normal and wondered if he'd fallen asleep.

"Where were you tonight?" he asked suddenly.

"I took Nora out for a bite in town and to the movies."

"You didn't tell me you were going out." He was trying hard not to sound as if he'd been pouting, but she could tell otherwise.

"Sorry." She laughed. "I didn't know I needed to."

"I didn't say you needed to," he echoed, mimicking her slightly defensive tone. "It's just common courtesy, Rebecca. I missed you tonight at dinner…and Nora, of course."

Rebecca felt suddenly guilty for hurting his feelings, though she wasn't sure why.

"Nora wanted to bring you back some ice cream. Rocky Road," she admitted. "But I thought it would be too late to bother you."

"Are you always so sensible, Rebecca? Don't you know that it's never too late to wake somebody up for Rocky Road?" he asked, sounding amazed at her lack of life experience.

"Yes, I'm always sensible. It's one of my more annoying qualities," she informed him. "Would you like some ice cream? I could find some in the kitchen and get it for you."

"Don't bother. I was only teasing you." She couldn't quite make out his expression but sensed that she had cheered him up a bit and helped him get past the dark images.

He took her hand and held it between his two larger hands. "Do you know what I would really like right now?"

Something in his quiet, thoughtful tone set off alarm bells within her. "What's that?" she asked, feeling a giant lump form in her throat.

"I'd like to hold you... *Just* hold you," he said sincerely.

Rebecca's first thought was to bolt. Here it was, happening all over again, despite her best intentions for it not to. How did she get herself into these situations?

But something—some undefinable but totally potent force that had been working on her ever since she'd set eyes on this man—made her stay. And the longer she stayed, the more she imagined how wonderful it would feel to be held in Grant's arms, to be embraced by him and embrace him in return. And suddenly, all the loneliness and longing of so many empty years, feelings she had denied and kept carefully locked away in a secret place, came rushing in on her. She couldn't refuse Grant's simple request or deny herself a few moments of such simple satisfaction and contentment.

"Just holding. You promise?" she asked him.

"Absolutely," he replied. "I'm under the covers, you're on top. Completely and *totally* sensible. Wouldn't you agree?"

She nodded and sighed, a deep sigh of surrender and affection. "Very sensible," she replied.

Five

He opened his arms to her, and she moved into the circle of his strong, warm embrace. As she settled beside him, he turned toward her and physically coaxed her to curl against him. She dropped her head, then rested her cheek on his chest. She felt his chin graze the top of her head and his hand came up to stroke her hair. She vaguely recalled that she had gone to bed that night with her hair pulled back loosely in a ribbon. It seemed the ribbon was gone. Either it had fallen out or Grant had removed it.

It hardly mattered. She closed her eyes and savored the moment. She felt utterly at peace and totally complete. Here in the dark, in the middle of the night, listening to Grant's steady heartbeat and slow, deep breaths, she felt transported to a special place, as if together they'd created a private world.

"You have such wonderful hair," he murmured. "You look like a girl with it long and loose down your back like this. How old are you, anyway?" he asked suddenly.

Rebecca laughed. "Why do you want to know?"

"Why don't you want to tell me?" he replied, sounding vaguely amused. "I'm thirty-eight," he offered quite matter-of-factly.

"I know," she said simply. She knew his age from his medical records, though he looked much younger.

She was usually not shy at all about telling her age. But for some reason she felt reticent tonight.

"I don't think a woman should be asked to tell her age...or her weight," she said finally with an imperious air.

"I'd bet you're not even thirty yet," he guessed. "You're still a baby, Rebecca," he teased her. "A baby with a sassy tongue."

"I think that part of a compliment was mixed up in there someplace," she teased him in return. "So thanks...I guess."

"You're very welcome, I'm sure," he replied. His touch on her hair was so tender and loving, Rebecca realized it hardly mattered what he had said to her.

"Why don't you wear your hair like this more often?"

"Gets in my way when I work," she said simply.

"How about when you're not working? When you're going out on a date, for instance?"

Rebecca felt her body tense slightly at this line of inquiry. She wondered if she should lie and lead him to believe she had a boyfriend…or several. It might scare him off. But deception was not her. Besides, some part of her didn't want to scare him off.

"I don't date much," she admitted. "I usually work long hours and then need to take care of Nora."

"Of course you do." She felt him shrug. "But everyone has a social life."

She laughed. "I don't."

"I find that hard to believe," he persisted. "Men must ask you out all the time."

"I do get invitations," she admitted.

"But you're not involved with anyone right now?" he asked.

"There's been no one, really, since my divorce."

He was quiet for a moment. She felt his hand in her hair again and wondered what he was thinking. She itched to ask him about his romantic past, but didn't dare broach the subject—and doubtless ruin the mood.

"Your ex-husband must be a complete fool to have let you go."

"Yes, he is," she replied succinctly. Her blunt reply made Grant laugh.

"What happened? Another woman?" he asked quietly.

She nodded against his chest.

"The stupid jerk." The note of anger in his voice surprised her.

"It took some time, but I got over it."

"But not enough to try again," he reminded her.

She didn't reply. She knew why she felt so emotional all of a sudden. She hadn't talked so openly with a man in a long time. Longer than she could remember.

It was frightening to reveal herself to someone else. Terrifying, actually. Like jumping from a great height and trusting someone to catch her. But just as it would feel taking that leap, it was exciting as well to share secrets in the dark and to be entrusted with Grant's intimate truths. Maybe she had recovered from Jack's betrayal more than she'd guessed. Maybe getting to know Grant had helped her do that.

"It's all very much in the past for me," she said, and meant it. "My only concern now is that Jack, my ex-husband, is good to Nora."

"Is he?" Grant asked, sounding concerned.

"Jack isn't a bad guy. But he's a very self-centered person. He's always been that way. He's an attentive father when it's convenient for him. Otherwise..." Her voice trailed off. She didn't want to sound bitter. "Well, he tries, but he could do a lot better."

"Nora's a great kid. I don't know how any father could ever ask for more," Grant said sincerely. "You've done a great job with her, Rebecca. You should be very proud."

"Thank you. I am," Rebecca replied quietly. "It's one reason I can never really regret my marriage to Jack. If we hadn't married, I'd never have had Nora. No matter what, she's always the bright spot in my day."

"She's gotten to be the bright spot in my day, too," he said with a warm, low laugh. "Except for

you, Rebecca…when you're not being a slave driver,
I mean.''

"Thanks, I think." She laughed.

"Nora is the spitting image of you, you know.
Even her personality is a lot like yours. I bet you were
just like her growing up. I bet you grew up in a happy
family, too.''

His personal question about her background took
her by surprise. Mostly because she could tell from
his tone he'd been thinking about her, wondering
about her past. As she had been thinking about him.

"I was a lot like Nora, I guess. But I grew up with
two older sisters who spoiled me and bossed me
around a lot. We had a happy family, though. My
mother was a nurse, retired now. She worked part-
time until we were in high school. My father owned
a hardware store in our town.''

"Which was?''

"Guilford, Connecticut. It's a very small town on
the sound. It still hasn't changed much, though the
real estate values have gone through the roof since
the yuppies discovered it. But when I was growing
up there, it was really very quiet and off the beaten
track. And we were a very typical, average family, I
suppose,'' she added.

"Nothing about you is typical or average,'' he corrected her, his fingertip trailing against the line of her
cheek. "Your parents must be very special people, to
have raised you.''

"I think they're good people,'' she said quietly.

"But you'll have to meet them sometime and decide for yourself."

"I'd love to," he replied.

She wasn't sure why she'd added that last part. It had slipped out. It sounded silly to her once she'd said it. Of course Grant would never meet her family. How would that happen? It would have to be quite by accident, after she'd finished her work for him and their lives had gone on in two very separate paths.

"How about you?" she asked suddenly, wanting to shift attention from herself. "Did you and Matthew have a happy family life growing up?"

"We had everything kids could ask for, if that's what you mean. We went to private schools and spent summers out here, in this house. That was probably the best part of growing up for us," he replied quietly. "But our family wasn't really happy. My parents were both very successful and focused on their work. They never seemed to have much time for me and Matt…or make much time for us. But we got by. We had each other," he added on a brighter note.

Rebecca could tell he was trying to present an unhappy picture in the best light. Perhaps it was wrong of her, but she wanted to know more. She wanted him to feel open enough with her to show her the worst.

"That must have been hard for you," she said simply. "Children need to feel appreciated and loved. No matter how much they're given materially, it can't make up for a parent's time and love."

"Yes, that's very true," he agreed. "I'm not sure

why our parents ever married, actually, or bothered having children. They didn't get along and only stayed together for our sake.''

"Oh…that's too bad," Rebecca said. She understood so much more about him. "Are they still together?" she asked.

"My mother died when I was fourteen and Matt was nine. My father must have loved her, despite their problems, because he really grieved. He worked constantly once she was gone. Matt and I hardly saw him. But we grew even closer. So that was a plus.''

"I'm sorry to hear about your loss.''

"It was a shock when it happened. But that was a long time ago. In some ways, I suppose it made me stronger.''

Stronger? Or just more guarded and distant? For once, she managed to hold her tongue. No wonder he was having such a difficult time recovering from losing his fiancée, she realized. The recent tragedy had only reinforced the fears incurred by his earlier loss.

"I spent a lot of time looking after Matt. In some ways, I feel I raised him myself. More than my dad ever did. But now, the roles are completely reversed,'' he observed with a harsh laugh. "The kid's doing a pretty damn good job, though, I think.''

"Yes, he is,'' Rebecca agreed. She was glad Grant had shared his unhappy memories with her but sad to learn he'd suffered so much emotional damage growing up. She had an urge to soothe him and comfort him for those long past hurts. But she chided herself for the impulse. She'd asked him personal questions, and he'd answered her. He wasn't asking for her comfort or sympathy. He'd probably be appalled by such a reaction.

They lay together silently for what seemed to Rebecca a long time. She wondered if Grant was falling asleep. Yet his hand still moved restlessly through her hair and up and down her back.

The warm, steady pressure of his touch was tender and soothing, lulling her into a sleepy state. But she knew she couldn't fall asleep in his bed. Good heavens! That wouldn't do. She knew she had to go, the sooner the better. But her body felt so warm and relaxed, tucked against Grant's hard, muscular form, it was hard to budge.

"I guess, because of the way I grew up, for a long time I just didn't get it about marriage and kids," he said finally. "Especially about the children. Oh, I thought it was nice enough for other guys I knew to settle down and start a family. But secretly, I always thought, 'Gee, another poor sap got himself caught. I'm too smart for that.' I know it sounds cynical, but I just couldn't understand why any guy in his right mind would tie himself down that way."

"Well, at least you're honest," Rebecca replied. It was shocking but certainly refreshing to hear a man make such blatant admissions. Most men she met were willing to say anything to get a woman into bed. But when it was time to make a commitment, their story changed quite a bit.

"Back then, I suppose I kept telling myself I was just waiting for the right woman to come along."

Rebecca lifted her head and pulled away from him enough to see his face.

"Then the right woman did come along." She forced herself to speak. She was referring to Courtney.

He was silent. She felt her throat go suddenly tight. He was about to start talking about Courtney. She had encouraged him. Yet she wasn't sure she could handle it.

Still, there was no earthly reason she should feel so upset and unsettled to hear him reminisce about the woman he had loved. Still loved, probably. Maybe Rebecca was lying in his arms right now, but this stolen hour together was nothing more than a bit of friendly comfort for him, wasn't it? A chance to clear his head from his terrifying dreams. Dreams about losing Courtney.

"No," he said finally. "It wasn't quite like that. I realized what I was missing out on well before I met Courtney. I'm not sure how it happened, really. One day I just knew I had enough—enough money, enough success, enough exotic trips, enough dinners at fancy restaurants and late nights out at exclusive clubs."

Wow, what a lifestyle he'd enjoyed. Rebecca's mind reeled. A far cry from her leisure hours, which usually contained a pizza and a rented video.

"It all came to a head one year during the holidays. You're supposed to be so happy and cheerful. But I felt awfully down that year. Matthew was in California on business, and I didn't have any plans or anyone to spend Christmas day with. I was dating a model at the time—''

A model. Rebecca silently moaned. *Please, spare me the details.*

''She was off on a shoot somewhere hot and tropical. She asked me to join her, but I didn't want to, so I guess that says it all about that affair.''

Rebecca suddenly felt much better. At least he found the model boring. It was some consolation.

''Anyway,'' he continued, ''here I was, feeling pretty sorry for myself, when I ran into an old college buddy—you know, one of those poor saps I was telling you about. I don't know how it happened, but I ended up going to his house for Christmas Eve. It was a big party, with a lot of family and friends, so I didn't stick out quite as much as I had feared. He had a great wife and two adorable kids. It was fun watching them tear open their presents,'' he added.

Rebecca could tell from his voice how much the experience had affected him. Even now, the memories of that visit were still very vivid for him, she could tell.

''I remember the ride back to the city. I couldn't believe it. This college chum, who I'd never thought was very sharp or had amounted to much, suddenly looked like the smartest, richest, most successful guy in the world. I would have changed places with him in a second. It was like a lightbulb going off inside my head. A big lightbulb. Then I realized how for so long I'd felt empty and bored. Yet I didn't understand what was missing in my life. Making a real commitment, having a true partner to share the ups and downs. Raising a family. That was it. The answer I'd been looking for.'' He was quiet. ''Then Courtney came along, and it all fell into place for us, more or less. And I had a chance to have what I really wanted out of life. But now I guess I'll never have that chance again.''

The light, conversational tone of his voice could not completely mask his sadness and pain. Rebecca wasn't sure what to say. There seemed no answer to his dilemma, and yet she knew in her heart that the only thing keeping Grant from having the life he'd once dreamed of was his will, his thwarted perspective.

''I'm sorry...I must be boring you,'' he apologized.

''No, not at all,'' she assured him. ''I was just thinking about what you said at the end, how it's all lost for you. It's not, you know. Only if you want it to be.''

''Please, Rebecca. It's been so good to talk with you like this tonight. I don't want to end up in an argument. This is the way I feel, and by God, I can't help it.''

His voice held a harsh note, and she braced herself. She feared she'd made him angry.

''I'm sorry. I didn't mean to upset you.'' She was sorry, but she wouldn't contradict herself and agree with him to soothe his feelings. She'd only told him the simple truth.

''Listen, I know you're only trying to make me feel better. But unfortunately, it doesn't work that way.

Even if I could some day get over my feelings about Courtney and the accident—which I don't believe will ever happen—I don't know if I could ever take that…that leap again. I'd be too afraid of losing someone I loved. Too afraid of some awful unforseen event taking everything away from me.''

His voice was so quiet and bleak, Rebecca instinctively moved closer. Maybe it was best not to argue with him. But she couldn't keep from saying what was on her mind.

"I know what you're saying. It's understandable that you'd feel this way. But I want to ask you one thing. You don't have to answer me. I think you should ask yourself, if the situation had been reversed, if you had died in the accident and Courtney had survived, would you want her to live the rest of her life alone? Without a husband or children?''

"No, of course not," he said adamantly. "I'd never wish that for her…for anyone.''

"Then why are you wishing it on yourself?" she asked bluntly.

He stared at her as if the truth of her words was sinking in. Then he shook his head. "You don't understand, Rebecca. It's just not the same. I was driving the car. I caused the accident that took her life…and our child's. It was all my fault.''

"Was it? There was a terrible storm that night. The road was treacherous. Maybe you skidded to avoid another car, or maybe you hit a bad stretch of pavement. You don't know for a fact that it was your fault, Grant," she reminded him.

"That's the problem…I can't remember. Not about the actual accident or much of the time right before it." He rubbed his forehead. "Except when I have one of these horrible nightmares, and then everything is so dark and distorted it's impossible to tell what's a real memory and what's just part of the dream. If only I could remember."

"Well, even if you do, what then? Would you be blaming yourself for not avoiding someone who stopped short in front of you or a cat who ran into the road? You're not superhuman you know Grant. An accident like that could happen to anyone."

"Yes, I know that rationally, Rebecca…but it's not the way I feel deep inside. In here," he added, touching the middle of his chest. "I blame myself for what happened. And because I do, I don't believe I'll ever be free to truly love again. Maybe I'm just afraid. Afraid of what might happen now that I've lived through the worst. Isn't that what you're trying to tell me?"

"Grant, no, that's not what I mean. It's not what I mean at all."

"Or maybe I believe I don't deserve a second chance after what I did. I know that's not rational, either, Rebecca. But maybe that's just the way I really feel."

Her mouth opened to reply. Then she could see it was useless to argue with him.

"If you say so, then I guess that it must be so," she finally agreed. "But whether it's fair or true is another story, I suppose."

"Another story for another day," he replied in a tone that warned her to let the topic go. "Some day, a long time from now, maybe I'll feel differently... And my future—what's possible for me—will look a great deal different, too."

"Maybe," Rebecca said wistfully. "I truly hope so."

"So do I," he replied. "So do I."

He swallowed hard and lifted his hand to cup her cheek. He met her gaze and stared deeply into her eyes. She thought he wanted to say something more. Something important.

But Rebecca abruptly broke the silence. "I need to go now. I've stayed way too long."

He looked sorry to hear she wanted to leave, but his expression quickly turned to one of resignation.

"Yes, of course. You'd better return to your own bed. If anyone finds you here, they might get the right idea about us."

"The *wrong* idea, you mean," she corrected him.

"Oh, right. The *wrong* idea. That's what I meant to say," he assured her with a teasing grin.

Before releasing her, he leaned over and kissed her softly. His warm mouth lingered tenderly. She knew he was savoring the taste and feel of her lips against his, hinting at unimaginable pleasures.

But the kiss ended as quickly as it had begun. Much too quickly, Rebecca thought.

He pulled away with a soft, reluctant sigh, and she stood up and looked at him. Sitting back against the pillows, his arms folded behind his head, his chest bare and the sheet draped around his waist, he was so impossibly handsome and appealing to her, she didn't know if she had the willpower to go.

"Well...good night," she said in a tender whisper. "I hope you won't have any more bad dreams."

He smiled softly. "No chance of it now. I'll only have sweet dreams of you...but not as frustrating as our real-life encounters, I hope," he added with a sexy grin.

Rebecca felt herself blush, and with another quick good-night she left the room.

In the hall, she wasn't sure which way to turn—toward her bedroom or the kitchen. After nearly an hour in Grant's bed, she did really need something to calm her down so she headed for the kitchen.

She sipped her tea, but it didn't soothe her ragged nerves very much. Her mind was filled with Grant and his intimate confessions. Despite his argument to the contrary, she did believe that someday, his feelings about the accident and losing Courtney would change. If he wanted them to.

But would it be too late? Too late for Grant to rejoice in love, marriage and children—those deeply satisfying experiences he valued far above success and material possessions.

And more important, would it be too late for anything serious to develop between them, as well?

Yes, it probably would be too late. It hurt to admit the truth, even to herself.

The conversation had ended painfully for both of them. But it had been an eye opener. She understood him far better now, and it was all for the best that she knew any secret hopes of romance between herself and Grant were vain and foolish fantasies.

Maybe that was why he'd confided in her so openly. Consciously or unconsciously, he'd wanted her to know he wasn't able to become emotionally involved with her. Not in a real relationship, one that would stretch beyond their time together as therapist and patient.

He was healing on the outside. But inside, Rebecca realized sadly, he still had a long way to go.

Six

Grant woke at dawn without the aid of his alarm clock. Soft sunlight filtered into his room, and before he opened his eyes, he heard the raucous sea gulls cruising the beach for their breakfast.

He liked to wake up early these days, and he never slept with the curtains pulled closed anymore. As he opened his eyes and slowly stretched, he smiled, anticipating the day. He had promised to meet Nora on the beach this morning and teach her how to surf cast. He had spent hours after dinner last night preparing their equipment, testing the reels on old fishing rods and rethreading the lines. He hoped the fish were jumping this morning. By heavens, if he could bribe somebody to stock the shoreline behind his house, he would, just for the pleasure of seeing Nora's adorable little face light up when she felt that first real tug.

He leaned over and checked the clock. It was only half past five. He didn't need to rush. He took a deep breath and realized he felt happy this morning. Happy to be alive. Happy to wake and stretch his arms and legs without feeling pain. Well, a cramp or two perhaps, but nothing like before. He was inordinately pleased to know he could sit up, swing his legs off the side of the bed and stand on his own two feet. With the aid of a cane, he could get just about wherever he wished to go.

He was starting to feel his old self again. And, in some mysterious, unfathomable way, not just his old self, but a new self. A better self. He had always imagined that once he'd reached this point in his recovery, he'd be rushing to the city, diving headlong into the mayhem of Wall Street.

But he felt no pressure to return to the madness and competition. From a distance, it looked so senseless to him, like so many eager rats, futilely running on their little wheels. Getting no place fast. All in the pursuit of money and more money. He once felt that being rich was the only true measure of success. But he felt differently now. Very differently. Not to mention that he had enough money to last several lifetimes.

And if he sometimes missed the mental challenge and stimulation of his work, he could keep up with everything he needed to know from here. The high-flying world of finance was no farther away than his computer.

The nightmares still returned from time to time. And bad headaches, as well. But each time he was plunged into that dark world he emerged with some precious fragments of his lost memories. He was keeping a journal, a private notebook where he tried to record the images before they faded. From time to time, when he felt strong enough, he looked through the scribbled notes and tried to piece the bits together. Sometimes he felt on the verge of remembering. Then something held him back, some force so strong he'd feel physically ill, dizzy and shaken and short of breath, trying to remember.

The doctors had told him he shouldn't try to force it. His memory would return in its own time, in its own way, they said. Yet Grant felt an irresistible compulsion, a driving need to remember that night, to remember everything that had happened to him in that car until the moment of impact.

He wasn't sure why he felt so compelled to remember. Many people would prefer to forget, he guessed. Sometimes he wondered if he was trying to torture himself. To punish himself for recovering, for feeling better and starting to take some simple pleasure in life again.

But other times, he had a more positive view. He saw it as a search for a key that would unlock both his missing past and his future. For without those lost hours and true understanding of the tragedy that had befallen him, he believed he could never be totally free of the grief and the guilt he carried.

His hand slipped under his pillow, and he felt the satin ribbon he had hidden there. He took it out and looked at it, curled it in the palm of his hand. It was apricot in color and frayed a bit on one end. He'd die before he'd ever let anyone know he kept it there. It was Rebecca's ribbon. It had fallen out of her hair the night she'd come to his bed and lain in his arms. He'd discovered it the next morning, a wonderful surprise. He'd thought of returning it to her, then knew he never would. He had to have it, a precious souvenir of their hours together.

That night had been so special to him. A turning point in his recovery, he believed, though he'd never told her so. Although they had not shared physical intimacy, he'd felt closer to her that night than to almost anyone he'd ever known. Grant knew very well that he could share his body with a woman without the experience being the least bit intimate or personal. Rebecca was different. With just a smile or a glance, she never failed to touch his soul.

It had been at least three weeks ago, and he'd struggled like hell to keep his hands off her. He knew she was wondering why, after sharing such tender intimacy, he suddenly chose to keep a cool, polite distance between them. But the reason was simple. He didn't dare let himself fall in love with her. He knew he was already falling. He knew his feelings for her ran very strong and deep. But somehow he hoped he could manage to keep them under wraps until her work here was done. He hoped he could keep her from growing more attached than she might feel already. And though he fantasized endlessly about truly loving her and knowing that she returned his love, it was a dream from which he was always harshly awakened.

He rolled the ribbon in his hand and crushed it into

a small ball. How could their relationship ever work out? It couldn't.

He had the world to offer her and Nora in a material sense, but nothing to offer Rebecca emotionally. Though he was almost healed physically, he knew he remained broken and damaged. He was hideously scarred inside, a monster no woman could ever really love.

Rebecca deserved so much more. She deserved the very best of men, not the worst. She deserved someone free to love her completely, without shadows of the past hovering over her happiness. No, he was damaged goods. Damaged beyond repair, perhaps. Still, Rebecca gave him hope. Hope of recovering physically, and in more optimistic moments, hope of somehow working through the demons that plagued his soul.

The summer was passing day by day. Minute by minute, hour by hour, his precious time with Rebecca was coming to an end. Every day he grew stronger, every step he took on his own was another step he took away from her. He knew it. And she knew it, too.

At times, he regretted the fact that he hadn't made love with her that night. How easy it would have been to pull her close and kiss her. How easily their kisses would have turned to something more. God, he would have adored every inch of her. He would have made love to her as she'd never been loved before.

But then what? Once she'd returned to her ever-sensible self, there would have been hell to pay. She probably would have quit on him. Left him flat. And he would have felt horrible for taking advantage of her attraction to and affection for him. Now there was something new about him. In the past, he could rarely recall feeling guilty for making a move on a willing woman. Had he developed a conscience with all these extra muscles Rebecca had put on him?

He could never use Rebecca for the purposes of a one-night stand, a casual, convenient affair that would end once she left the house. He knew women very well. Too well, he thought at times. Rebecca was definitely not the type for a quick fling. She was the type a man cherished for a lifetime. Anything less would hurt her deeply. And he would never hurt her, not for the world. Not even in exchange for the pleasure of making love to her, which he was sure would be heavenly. He gazed at the ribbon and touched it to his lips. She would never be in his bed again. Of that, he was sure. The hours they'd shared together were a special gift, a stolen, guilty pleasure. And that was all there would be, no matter how it tortured him to hold her at arm's length. Maybe that was why the ribbon seemed so precious. He knew he'd never get physically close to her again, though in his heart, he'd treasure her for a lifetime.

Sometimes, when Grant found himself lost in thoughts of Rebecca, he felt a sudden pang, thinking he was being unfaithful to Courtney. He stared at her picture on his night table. If he was totally and coldly honest with himself, he knew he could barely recall any deep, soul-stirring feelings for Courtney. He remembered their mutual strong attraction and common interests, common friends. He remembered an affectionate, warm feeling toward her. Even a possessive feeling. But it was nothing like the feelings he held for Rebecca. Had he ever really loved Courtney? he wondered. Maybe his feelings for her were one more item lost to his memory. Yet, if all he had felt was what he could remember…well, it seemed disrespectful to Courtney's memory, Grant had to recognize that his feelings for his past love seemed pale and superficial compared to his feelings for Rebecca. Feelings that grew stronger each moment he spent with her. Emotions that seemed to penetrate to the marrow of his bones, to his very soul.

Courtney, did I ever know that kind of love for you? he silently asked the picture. Of course, the blond, blue-eyed image posed no answer. She stared at him, frozen in time. Lost to him forever. On impulse, he picked up the photo and slipped it into a drawer.

The sunlight was stronger. It streamed into the room and warmed his bare skin as he sat at the edge of his bed. Time to get moving. It wasn't polite to keep ladies waiting. Nora and Rebecca, no less. Rebecca would give him the sharp side of her tongue if she'd got up at dawn for this outing and he dawdled. He smiled, anticipating her sassy remarks.

Yes, it could be a wonderful day, he told himself, *if you let it.*

The surf-casting lesson was a great success. Grant hardly minded having to sit in a wheelchair to be stable enough to fish. He knew he'd progressed far beyond the chair, and it was only a precaution. Besides, sitting in the chair, he was able to hold Nora on his lap and help her with her fishing line. When they felt a mighty tug, he savored the expression on her face—so much so that he lost focus on the line, and the reel spun like crazy.

When they finally got the pole under control, he and Nora battled their prize catch together. At one point, the fish pulled so hard, they felt the wheelchair rolling toward the shoreline. Luckily, Rebecca caught them before they were pulled in. Nora thought a ride into the pounding surf on a runaway wheelchair was terrific fun, and after their initial shock, Rebecca and Grant had a good laugh.

Finally, the fishing lesson ended and they made their way to the house, feeling tired, hungry and happy. Nora insisted on carrying the fish they'd caught in a pail of ice and water, though the load was heavy for her. She and Grant had reeled in a huge bluefish, a real beauty, he thought. He couldn't wait to get to the house and take a picture of Nora holding up her catch.

Rebecca had caught some small fish and tossed them back. Grant could see that fishing would never be her favorite pastime, but she was a good sport and got just as excited as Nora when the bluefish was landed.

Once they'd all cleaned up, they gathered for breakfast in the kitchen. Grant had rarely eaten a meal in the kitchen in all the years he'd spent in this house. But lately, since he'd been able to amble around on a cane, he'd started cooking again, and it seemed convenient and cozy to have Rebecca and Nora with him in the kitchen while he played master chef and they followed his orders or simply sat chatting, waiting to be fed.

This morning, he made waffles with fresh fruit. As Nora carried the platter to the table, Rebecca rubbed her hands together in hungry anticipation.

"Yum, my favorite," she said, hungrily eyeing the platter. "Pass that platter right here to Mom, darling," she teasingly coaxed Nora. She helped herself to a waffle and all the trimmings. He liked to see her enjoying the food he cooked. That was half the fun. "With all the fuss you made over that fish, Grant, I was half-afraid I was going to experience my first blue fish omelette."

"I'm saving that beauty for dinner. I was thinking of a mustard sauce." He was about to describe some recipes he had in mind when Nora interrupted him.

"You're going to cook it?" she squeaked. "You're going to cook my fish?"

Grant and Rebecca stared at her. Grant glanced at Rebecca, not knowing how to handle this delicate situation.

"Well, what do you think we should do with it, Nora?" he asked her very seriously.

"I don't know." Nora shrugged. He could see the tears in her eyes, but she valiantly held them back. She stared down at her waffle. "But I didn't think we were going to eat it."

"But honey, I thought you knew that's what people did with the fish they catch," Rebecca said.

Nora shrugged again. Grant caught Rebecca's eye.

"Listen, Nora, would you feel better if we put the fish back in the ocean?"

She lifted her head, and he knew from her expression that he'd hit pay dirt. "Can we? I thought it was dead. I thought we killed it once we took it out of the ocean."

"Well, we left it in a pail of cold water outside. Maybe it's still breathing. Let's go check."

Walking at a slow pace behind Nora, Grant sent up a silent prayer that the glorious bluefish was still breathing and would be strong enough to live if they tossed it back in the waves.

With his fingers crossed, Grant peered into the pail over Nora's slim shoulder. By golly, it looked good. Very good. The fish was flipping and flapping about with loads of life left in it.

Without more conversation, they returned to the beach and Grant had the honor of flinging the fish far out over the breakers. They stood silently watching. Rebecca shielded her eyes against the sun with her hands.

"I think you threw it far enough," she said finally.

"I hope so." Grant watched the shoreline to see if the fish had been caught in a wave and dashed toward the beach. He didn't see it pulled back in.

"I think he's swimming home as fast as he can," Nora said. "He wants to tell his family how he got caught by some big ugly humans and they nearly ate him for dinner. With mustard sauce. But somehow, he escaped."

Rebecca and Grant laughed at her story. Grant reached out and playfully tugged Nora's braid. "I'm sure that fish is bragging all over the Atlantic about his clever escape," Grant agreed. "Feel better?" he asked kindly.

She nodded, then impulsively flung her arms around Grant's waist and hugged him tight. Grant hugged her as best as he could, balanced precariously on his cane. "There now...what's this all about?"

"Thank you," she said, lifting her head.

"You're welcome," he replied. "Hey, but I never got a picture of you with that fish," he said regretfully. "I was looking forward to saving it in my album."

"I'll draw you one at camp today," she promised.

"Deal," he replied with a wide smile..

They shook hands in a very official manner, and when Grant caught Rebecca's warm, admiring grin, his heart swelled with warmth and affection for both of them.

After Nora left for camp, Grant and Rebecca met in the exercise room for Grant's daily workout. Grant arrived a bit early and began his requisite stretches. Rebecca entered and spared him a quick, approving smile. While she moved around the room, checking the equipment, Grant took the opportunity to check her out.

The day had warmed up considerably since the early morning fishing adventure, and Rebecca was dressed in white cotton shorts, a ribbed black tank top and white running shoes. Her hair, which she usually wore in a ponytail or long braid, was loose today, pulled back from her face with a wide black hair band that emphasized her high cheekbones, large, hazel eyes and thick dark lashes.

She looked wonderful, he thought. Absolutely. But seemingly not conscious of it at all. He'd never met a woman who was so naturally beautiful yet so unaware of her good looks. Or the effect she had on a man.

Seated on the floor, Grant took a deep breath, leaned forward and reached for his toes. Her shorts were very short, he thought, greedily taking in an eyeful of her gorgeous long legs. As his gaze surreptitiously traveled upward, he couldn't help but notice that the tank top she wore was a bit skimpy. He didn't remember seeing it on her before. Perhaps it was new. Was he imagining it, or was it tighter and cut a bit lower than the tops she usually wore?

With her back toward him, she leaned over and picked up some hand weights. He swallowed hard. She was gorgeous. Sometimes he wanted her so badly it hurt. This was going to be an extra difficult session to get through, he realized, gritting his teeth.

His consternation and distress must have shown on his face, he realized, for when she turned to him she met his gaze with a curious stare. "Are you all right?" she asked with innocent concern.

"I'm fine," he insisted. Holding the exercise table for support, he pulled himself to a standing position.

"You looked like something hurt while you were doing the stretches," she replied, walking toward him. "Any pain or soreness?"

"No, not at all." He crossed his arms. "Let's get on it with it, shall we? I have work to do today. I can't spend the day in here like some mindless bodybuilder."

"My, my, aren't we cranky today," Rebecca replied lightly as she scanned the notations on her clipboard. "Anything you'd like to talk about?"

"I just have things on my mind, that's all," he explained abruptly. "Work...other things."

He certainly couldn't confess to her that his foul mood was largely due to his effort to keep her at a safe distance. If he didn't keep up a solid defense of grouchiness and sarcasm, he might give way to the temptation to pull her into his arms and make passionate love to her right on the exercise table.

She watched as he got on the treadmill and gripped the hand supports. "You must be eager to get back to work now that you're doing so much better," she said.

"Sometimes I am," he admitted. *But not for the reasons you might think, Rebecca. Sometimes I wish I was back at my desk because the bedlam of my demanding job would provide some distraction from my longing for you.*

"Well, it won't be too much longer. You're improving every day," she replied.

He glanced at her. She was fiddling with some settings on the machine, and he couldn't see her expression.

Her voice had sounded so cool and impersonal, he would have thought the idea of their time together ending meant little to her. Yet he didn't believe that. Maybe she felt as badly as he did about their relationship. Sometimes he thought she was angry at him for drawing her so close that night she came to his bedroom, then pushing her away. For showing her a glimpse of how wonderful it could be between them, then taking that treasure from her. Maybe she felt rejected by him and didn't realize that keeping his distance was the only way he knew how to protect her, to save her from some far greater pain that following through on their feelings for each other would surely cause down the road.

"That reminds me. I'm going to test you today to gauge your progress. Then maybe I can give you some approximate date in regard to returning to your office."

He met her gaze. Her expression was calm and poised, but in her eyes, he saw a flash of sadness and regret. He longed to reach out to her, to frame her lovely face in his hands and kiss her tempting lips. To promise her he'd never leave her, if that's what she wished.

But of course, he couldn't do that. He couldn't act on any part of his fantasy. He turned and faced forward, gripping the support railing. "Sounds good to me," he replied.

She checked to see that he was ready to begin, then turned on the machine and carefully noted his distance and speed. They went through the rest of the exercise circuit with little conversation.

After they completed the cooldowns and more stretching, Rebecca carefully measured flexibility and range of motion on Grant's injured leg. It was absolute torture for him to sit still and remain relaxed as she handled his body with her soft, tender touch. When she saw his grim expression, he thought she mistook his effort at self-control as an effort to hide physical pain.

But soon enough, the sweet torture was over and Grant sat sipping a large bottle of water while he watched Rebecca review the notations on her chart. She was concentrating, jotting notes here and there, flipping through pages to check records. He could watch her for hours, he thought. He just loved looking at her.

Finally, she looked up to find him grinning at her. He could tell she was trying hard not to smile, and finally she couldn't help herself.

"What's so funny?" she asked him.

"Nothing." He shrugged and took a long cooling sip of water. "I just like watching you try to tally me up and figure me out."

"I could never figure you out," she assured him. "I won't even waste my time trying."

He laughed. "Oh, I think you do a lot better than you give yourself credit for, Rebecca," he answered with a grin. "A lot better than most women I've known," he added.

"Well, thanks. But that's not saying much," she muttered, looking at his chart.

"So, how did I do? Am I ready for the Olympics?"

"Definitely. The wise guy competition. I'm sure you'll stun the judges," she replied dryly.

He laughed heartily and again fought the urge to pull her into his arms. "No, seriously, Rebecca. What's the bottom line here?"

"I need to look at these records closer, of course, but it all looks very good to me. I think that if there are no unforseen setbacks for the next few weeks, you should be able to return to work after Labor Day.''

A slight smile played at the corners of her mouth, but it didn't reach her eyes. Her pleasure at delivering this piece of good news was bittersweet, he could see. He knew how she felt, for he felt exactly the same. He sat quietly, taking it all in, then he saw that she was puzzled by his lack of obvious reaction.

''Aren't you happy?'' she asked him quietly. ''You did say back in May that your goal was to return to work by the end of the summer.''

''Yes, I remember,'' he answered. ''I guess it's sort of a shock to hear that it will finally happen. Maybe I've gotten lazy and grown too comfortable living the easy life out here,'' he added, trying to strike a lighter note.

''Maybe,'' she agreed, yet her tone sounded doubtful. ''You've made remarkable progress. You've worked very, very hard and have a lot to be proud of,'' she said sincerely.

The look in her eyes was almost his undoing. He swallowed hard and looked away. ''Thanks, Rebecca,'' he said simply. ''That means a great deal to me, coming from you. I couldn't have done it without you. I remember how you marched in here that first day, yanked open those curtains and told me I was wallowing in self-pity.''

''I opened the curtains, but I never said such a thing to you,'' she denied.

''You didn't have to say it. I could see it in your eyes, as plain as day. It made me feel ashamed of myself, thank God. I sometimes wonder what would have happened to me if you had never come along. I'd probably still be sitting in that chair, in that dark room, feeling miserable and sorry for myself. And making everyone around me miserable, too.''

''You were ready to help yourself,'' she insisted. ''I just gave you the means and a jump start.''

More than that, Rebecca, he longed to say. *So much more. Your smile gave me a reason to get out of bed every morning.*

But he restrained himself from confessing his feelings. Instead, he glanced away from her and tugged on the towel that was slung around his neck.

''And don't forget a good tongue-lashing when I didn't push myself to meet your standards…Your Highness.''

''That, too,'' she replied, smiling at him warmly. She crossed her arms and regarded him in a way that made his heart race. He was glad she was done checking his pulse and blood pressure for the day. He imagined his readings would jump off the chart.

''Listen, before I go I want to thank you for what you did for Nora this morning, Grant,'' she said finally.

''Taking her fishing? That was no trouble. I loved every minute, even when the wheelchair nearly rolled into the ocean.''

Rebecca laughed. ''That was a close call, wasn't it? I think you need a life preserver tied on the back of that thing.''

''Maybe, or an outboard motor,'' he joked.

''Actually, I didn't mean the fishing, though it was fun. I meant later, when she got upset. Even I didn't understand what was going on with her. It was very sweet of you to talk to her the way you did and figure out what was bothering her. She's waiting to hear if her father will be visiting for her birthday this week, and I guess she's a little sensitive right now.''

"I hope he comes," he replied.

"Yes, so do I. We should hear from him tonight. But it was nice of you, all the same."

She gazed at him with gratitude for the consideration he'd shown her child, and Grant felt overwhelmed. He felt so proud that he had won the respect of this very special woman. It had seemed such a small gesture on his part, but she obviously thought otherwise. If only she knew how much he would do for her and Nora if he were able. He'd give them both the world.

Finally, he couldn't resist touching her. He reached out and took her hand, holding it in both of his.

"It was nothing. You don't need to thank me. I'm crazy about Nora. You must know that by now."

"Yes, I know. And she's crazy about you, too," she confessed. He felt the answering grip of her hand, and the sensation raced along his limbs like a brush fire. "But I worry about it sometimes, to be honest. I mean, we won't be here forever."

"She's getting too attached to me...is that the problem?" he asked quietly.

"Something like that."

"Don't worry," he assured her. "I'm not your ex-husband. I won't disappoint her if I can ever help it."

He rested his hands on her shoulders, and when she

wouldn't look at him, he gently lifted her chin with his fingertips.

"Didn't you hear what I said, Rebecca?" he asked quietly.

She looked upset, her eyes shining with unshed tears. She nodded, seeming too moved to speak.

"Yes, I heard you," she answered finally. "It's just that maybe you won't be able to help it. Maybe we don't mean to hurt someone we care about, but sometimes we just can't help it."

Her words struck a deep note in his heart. She seemed to be talking more about herself than about her daughter. He knew she had struggled to understand why he had set up an invisible barrier between them since their night together. She had struggled to understand and had tried her best not to blame him. Still, it had hurt.

He had no choice. He couldn't stop himself from kissing her and holding her tight, from stealing a few precious minutes of paradise in her arms. His head dropped, and their lips met. He felt her resistance for an instant, then he felt her relax and melt into his arms. Her mouth opened under the pressure of his, and he heard a small sigh of satisfaction deep in her throat that thrilled him down to the marrow of his bones.

Their kiss went on and on, his tongue plundered the honey sweetness of her soft, warm mouth in a mindless foray of tasting and savoring. His hands roamed up and down her sleek body, stroking her breasts through the thin fabric of her tank top and then moving, to the silky bare skin at the hem of her shorts. His hands moved around her hips and gently cupped her bottom, pulling her against his building heat.

He heard her groan with desire as their bodies pressed tightly together, heat seeking heat. He was ready to make love to her. He kissed her deeply, bending her head back as he nearly robbed her of her breath. Leaning against the wall for support, he held her tightly and turned her slightly to the side, slipping his hand between her smooth, lean thighs, then stroking her most sensitive and intimate place. She sighed, her hips rising to meet his rhythmic touch, then she shuddered with pleasure in his arms. She seemed half inclined to break away and half inclined to ask for even more.

He gazed at her beautiful face. While one hand continued to caress her lower body, his mouth covered the peak of one breast, his tongue swirling in lazy circles around her hardened nipple. He heard her moan and sigh, felt her move restlessly against him and finally felt her fingertips dig into his shoulder as he absorbed the tremors of excitement that rocked her slender body.

He longed to be inside her, to love her completely and bring her to the very height of pleasure, to give her everything he had to give and more. To make love to her like no man had ever loved her before.

"Rebecca, Rebecca," he sighed, raining soft kisses on her cheeks, her closed eyelids and her soft lips. "God, I want you. I want you so much," he confessed.

She turned in his arms and buried her face in his

shoulder. Then she lifted her head and stared deeply into his eyes. "I want you, too," she admitted in a silken whisper. "But it's not right. It's not enough."

Her words were quietly spoken. But their impact was deep. Grant felt as if a door within him had opened for a moment, letting in fresh air and sunlight—and then, just as quickly, slammed shut.

He didn't know what to say. He let his hands linger on her waist and felt her slowly pulling away.

"I need to go now," she insisted.

"Okay." He nodded, his expression grim. "I'm sorry, Rebecca. Maybe I shouldn't have…"

She raised her hand and pressed her fingertips to his lips. "No, don't say that, please," she insisted. "It only makes it worse."

Ducking her head, she pulled away and swiftly left the room.

Grant sat alone at the long dining table, drumming his fingertips on the linen cloth. He'd spent the last half hour reading the newspaper but had grown bored with it and laid it aside.

He glanced around, suddenly conscious of the vast, banquet-size room. It seemed like an empty cavern stretching out around him, echoing his slightest movement or sound. Classical music floated through speakers hidden in the wall, and he rose stiffly, walked to the control and turned up the sound. Bach usually had a soothing effect on his nerves, but tonight not even Bach and a tumbler of premium Scotch whiskey calmed him while he waited for Rebecca and Nora to appear.

Mrs. Walker poked her head into the room. "Shall I have the maid serve, sir?" she asked quietly.

"Not yet." He glanced at his watch. "Let's give them another few minutes."

"Do you want me to call Ms. Calloway for you, sir?"

"No," he said abruptly. "That won't be necessary, Mrs. Walker, but thank you," he added more politely. "She did say she was coming down to dinner tonight, though, didn't she?" he asked, checking for perhaps the third time.

"Yes, she did, sir. I asked her myself this afternoon, when the cook needed to know how much food to prepare for the meal. She said she was planning on dining with you tonight."

"All right." He nodded, then carefully lowered himself into his chair. "I'll just wait then. Perhaps they were held up for some reason."

"Perhaps," Mrs. Walker agreed. Grant caught a flash of sympathy in her eyes. Feeling embarrassed, he looked away. "Can I bring you anything, sir?"

"No, thank you. I'll ring when I'm ready."

With a nod, Mrs. Walker retreated to the kitchen, and Grant was left alone again with his wandering thoughts. He had made a special effort with his appearance tonight, though he wasn't quite sure why.

After his shower, he had given himself an extra close shave and combed his hair carefully. Rebecca always teased him about needing a haircut, and for once, he was starting to believe her. He was wearing a collarless white linen shirt, khaki trousers and a navy blue blazer. When he glanced at his reflection in the mirror, he looked like his old self again. His before-the-accident self. Except for the thin scar that ran across his right cheek.

He touched it with his hand. He might have that removed someday. Someday soon. The doctor said it wouldn't take much. Though he'd never been one to fuss much with his looks, the scar was jarring whenever he caught sight of it. An unnecessary reminder of the accident.

As if he could ever forget that fateful night. He didn't need a scar on his face to remind himself, as he had once thought. The true scars were within, marks that no surgeon, however skillful, could ever erase.

He sighed and picked up the newspaper. He worried that he had scared Rebecca away with his ardent embrace this morning. He must have terrified her. He knew he'd terrified himself. If he could express that much explosive passion holding her for five minutes, fully clothed, what would happen if they ever made love? The question was nearly too much to contemplate.

Was she avoiding him on purpose, as she'd done in the past? Or was there some other reason for the delay? He checked his watch again. It was nearly half past seven, and she knew that dinner was served at seven sharp. He suddenly felt foolish. Surely she had a right to eat her dinner wherever she pleased. She didn't have to join him if it made her feel uncomfortable. She knew better than he did that whatever they felt for each other, however strong and real their feelings seemed to be, this was a temporary situation.

He would soon return to his office, to his life in the city and all the complications and distraction there that usually kept the loneliness and emptiness at bay. Rebecca would go on to another job in another house and work her special magic on some other needy soul.

He hoped to God her next patient wasn't a man. The thought of her tender, loving hands on some other man made his blood boil. But of course, that was inevitable, wasn't it? Once they went their separate ways, sooner or later she'd find someone to love. Some lucky man would find her. It was a miracle she was still unattached this long after her marriage. The men in New York City had to be either blind or just plain stupid, he thought bitterly.

Though it brought a sharp stab of pain to his injured leg, Grant stood abruptly and rang the dinner bell.

Mrs. Walker came running. "Yes, sir?" she inquired breathlessly.

"Have the maid serve, please. I don't think they're coming," he said simply.

"Yes, of course, sir. She'll be right in," Mrs. Walker replied. She paused in the doorway and turned to him. "Shall I have her clear the extra place settings?"

He glanced at the table. The empty chairs and place settings where Rebecca and Nora usually sat seemed to mock him. He felt sad and angry—mostly angry at himself for encouraging his vain hopes.

"Yes, clear them away," he said sharply. "Clear them right now."

"Yes, sir." Mrs. Walker hurried over carrying a silver tray and cleared the places herself.

Grant turned his back to her and sipped his whiskey and soda as he stared out the window. When he was finally alone again, he let out a deep sigh.

He tried to enjoy his food, a shrimp dish that was one of his favorites. But at every bite, he thought only of the bluefish they had returned to the sea. He skipped dessert and instead of returning to his rooms, he decided to walk on the beach.

The sun was setting and the horizon was tinged with color, deep lavender and amazing hues of gold and pink. As the sky in the east darkened, brilliant stars appeared.

He didn't see Rebecca and Nora sitting on a long driftwood log near the shoreline until he was only a few yards away. His first impulse was to turn and walk in the other direction. Then he realized that Nora wasn't leaning on her mother in a casual embrace, she was crying hard, and Rebecca was trying to soothe her.

He stopped and wondered what he should do. He didn't want to intrude on them, especially since their absence at dinner seemed to signify Rebecca didn't want his company tonight. Yet he felt concerned. Very concerned. Maybe there was something he could do to help, some problem he could solve. He thought he should at least offer his assistance.

Rebecca didn't notice him until he was standing right next to her. She looked up, clearly surprised. "Oh, Grant. It's you," she managed to say.

Nora didn't lift her head, but her crying did slow down a bit, Grant noticed.

"Is something wrong with Nora?" he asked quietly.

Rebecca stared at him, then looked away. The light wind blew wisps of hair across her cheek and mouth. He had the urge to brush them away but carefully restrained himself.

"Nora feels upset tonight. Very upset. That's why we didn't come to dinner," she added hurriedly. "Her father called and said he won't be able to make it back to New York this week for her birthday."

"Oh... That's too bad," Grant said sincerely.

He crouched in the sand next to them, not knowing what to say. Nora was sniffling, too embarrassed to look at him. He felt a pang in his heart, empathizing with her. His own father had disappointed him so many times in the same way—missing an important birthday, a big game, even his college graduation. Grant knew how it felt, how much it hurt. He had once promised himself that if he ever had children, he'd walk through fire to be there for them. He suddenly hated Rebecca's ex-husband for the heartless way he'd treated Nora...and for hurting Rebecca, as well.

"I've got an idea," he said on impulse. "Why don't we make that visit to New York City we were talking about. You know, when I promised to take you to the Plaza to see the portrait of Eloise?" he reminded her. "Do you remember?"

Nora slowly lifted her head. "Of course I remember," she replied.

She didn't smile, but she did look interested in the proposition, he noticed. He could feel Rebecca staring at him intently. He should have checked with her before blurting out the invitation, he realized. She probably would have opposed it.

"Can we really go there? For my birthday, I mean?" Nora said.

"Yes, definitely... If your mother says it's all right, of course," he added. He glanced at Rebecca and caught her eye. She looked furious but was holding back a smile, he could tell by the way the corner of her mouth twitched.

"Can I, Mommy? Please?" Nora begged.

"I guess you have to now," Rebecca replied, sounding cornered.

"Can my mom come, too?" Nora asked Grant.

"Of course. If she wants to. I for one would love to have her along. I could take you shopping to F.A.O. Schwartz...and take your mom down the street to Tiffany's," he teased.

"Come on, Grant. I won't go at all if you're going to joke like that," Rebecca replied.

"Who's joking?" he asked innocently.

"Cool!" Nora exclaimed as her bright blue eyes lit up. "My birthday is Friday. Can we go on the exact day?"

"Sure, why not? I'll make all the arrangements," Grant promised. "We'll stay in for the weekend at my place. There's plenty of room there for everyone."

"The weekend? I thought we'd just go in for the day," Rebecca said warily. Grant guessed that Rebecca knew very well about his place, a huge, duplex penthouse on the Upper East Side, with a view of

Central Park from one side and river views from the other. He would bet good money that Mrs. Walker, who sometimes worked there, had given Rebecca an earful about the city home. In her expression he could see her curiosity warring with something that looked like sheer terror at the mere mention of staying there. He wasn't at all surprised when she came up with a handy excuse.

"I'm sorry. It's a lovely invitation, really, and very generous of you, Grant, but we really can't stay over," she replied, not surprising him in the least.

"Oh, really? Why is that?" he asked calmly.

"Why can't we, Mommy? I really want to," Nora said.

"But you have to leave for your camping trip very early on Saturday morning," Rebecca reminded her. "The bus leaves at half past seven. We'll never make it back in time."

"Oh, that's right. I nearly forgot," Nora said to Grant. "I'm going on a real overnight in the woods, with my camp," she explained to him. "We're going to sleep outside in tents and everything."

"Sounds great," he said with a smile. He knew it would be a terrific experience for Nora, but he was sorry to learn that the trip put a damper on his plans. "Well, you'll have to visit my house in the city another time then, okay?"

"Of course we will," Nora promised brightly. "When we go back at the end of the summer. We'll all be back in New York then...right, Mommy?"

The mention of the end of their time together put a bittersweet twist on the conversation for Grant. He glanced at Rebecca and could tell she shared his feelings.

"Of course, we'll visit Grant sometime when we get back…if he wants us to," she added in a more tentative tone.

"Of course I do. But let's talk about Nora's birthday. We'll make a real day of it," he promised. "There's the Plaza and then maybe the Central Park Zoo." He began planning out loud. "Have you ever ridden in a helicopter, Nora? That would be something fun to do, don't you think?"

"A helicopter ride?" Rebecca exclaimed. He could see that the mere mention of it made her stomach lurch. "How about a plain old horse-drawn carriage?"

"I want to go in a helicopter, Mom," Nora insisted. "Wow, this is going to be great!" Nora jumped up and did a little jig in the sand. "This is going to be the greatest birthday I ever had."

"Guess I need to bring along some earplugs," Rebecca said as she shook her head and smiled.

"I believe they supply the earplugs," Grant offered. Nora held out her hands to him and pulled him. He smiled at her, holding her small hands in his as she danced around in the fading light. He felt like a hero, the ten-foot-tall variety, his injuries and shortcomings magically forgotten. It felt amazingly good to do something like this for Nora—and Rebecca, too, of course. He felt protective toward them…and needed.

Rebecca hugged her knees to her chest, and the long, loose sweater she was wearing slipped off one shoulder. Silhouetted against the sunset, he found her more beautiful and appealing than ever.

She tipped her head back and smiled at him, a secret smile that warmed his heart. She silently mouthed the words "Thank you."

"My pleasure," he silently answered.

It *would* be his pleasure, too. His utmost pleasure to show them the time of their lives. He knew only too well that they'd be parting soon enough…and forever. For despite what Rebecca had told Nora, he truly doubted they'd see each other in the city. He knew too well she'd only said so to appease Nora.

At least they'd have one special day together, something to look back on and treasure. The idea had been a gift from above, he suddenly realized.

One day would never be enough, of course. A thousand wouldn't satisfy him. But given the chance to spend this time with Rebecca and her daughter, he was determined to make it wonderful.

Seven

For the remainder of the week, Rebecca's head spun with doubts about spending a day in the city with Grant. It was a grand gesture on his part and a generous one. But carrying through on it made her feel obligated to him somehow.

Nora was so thrilled with the idea she talked of little else, and Rebecca didn't have the heart to call a halt to the outing. Especially since her ex-husband had almost ruined Nora's birthday entirely with his typical last-minute excuses.

It had been very kind of Grant to rush in and rescue the situation. More than kind, she knew. Even if he had wanted to cheer Nora up, she knew he hardly had to go so far out of his way to do so. He could have bought Nora a present or taken her into town for a movie or some special treat. When Rebecca considered the time, trouble and expense involved in the schedule he'd put together, she had to wonder why he was going to such lengths.

Well, he was a man with an active mind, and he was stirring with energy these days. Maybe planning this trip gave him something to do. A project for a man who had been burdened with responsibility not so long ago but lately had had none. Or maybe it was an easy way for him to get on his feet again, get reoriented to the city. He hadn't been to Manhattan, except to visit doctors, for months. Maybe he was wary about going back, and showing Nora around the town made it more palatable to him.

In more optimistic moments, she imagined his impulse sprang from deeper feelings—specifically, feelings for her. Maybe he felt more than mere attraction. Perhaps he had begun to see a future for them.

Then reality would sweep in like a giant wave, washing away all traces of her heart's lovely sand castles of hope. Yes, the attraction was real, mutual and as powerful as ever. But it still led nowhere, she reminded herself. Maybe to Grant's bed. But certainly not to a real relationship. Not as long as memories of the accident hung over him like a cloud. Or, to be more precise, his inability to remember the accident.

Even though they knew each other far better now, Rebecca feared that his attraction to her was still inspired by the reasons she'd suspected from the start— his need to regain his male confidence and his feelings of gratitude toward her for his recovery. Hadn't he admitted as much to her? He had told her he'd never have made it without her help. Hadn't that confession been voiced right before their last smoldering encounter, when his passionate kisses and persuasive touch had her ready and willing to make love with him atop the nearest horizontal surface?

Rebecca felt her cheeks grow warm just thinking about it. She'd behaved so wantonly, with such utter abandon, in his arms. She'd never responded quite that way to any man before Grant, and wondered if she ever would again. What would it be like to surrender finally to all the heat and hungry desire that simmered between them, to love him completely and feel his love in return? How many long hours she'd tossed in her bed this summer, fantasizing about that very question. Obsessing, she had to admit. He had become an obsession for her. She was stuck on him totally. He lived in her mind, in her heart, in her soul. She only hoped to heaven that once they were apart, her need for him would gradually fade, though she was sure the process would be a painful one. In light of her intense feelings, she often thought it had been a blessing they'd never made love. Wouldn't it be far worse for her later if they had? Or would it give her something of him to have and cherish in the lonely future? Rebecca was never sure of the answer.

Perhaps he'd try to persuade her to make love this weekend, while they were alone in the house with Nora and Matthew gone. For once, despite her levelheaded, ever-sensible side, Rebecca didn't know what she would do if that happened. Surely she could avoid him and hold the line for just a few more weeks. Surely, she could keep herself from having a real affair with him. He'd progressed so much this summer. He was gaining strength every day. He wouldn't need her much longer. They both realized that.

She knew she ought to see September as a light at the end of the tunnel. Yet having the end in sight made their remaining time together feel all the more precious, all the more intense and emotionally charged. For that reason and so many more, she felt wary of the upcoming weekend, when they would be alone together.

Her will to avoid an empty affair with Grant was strong. But she was only human. And probably—no, make that *definitely,* she mentally amended—totally in love with him. Did all her ethical, logical reasons to resist him stand a chance against those odds?

Rebecca couldn't help but feel nervous on Friday morning as she and Nora got ready to meet Grant. She fussed more than usual over Nora's outfit and her hair until even her typically even-tempered daughter had to complain.

Grant had the car waiting for them at the front of the house, and they were already five minutes late. But Rebecca couldn't get her hair right. For some reason, it wouldn't stay where she pinned it in a neat French roll. As she pulled the pins out and attempted to fix it, Nora tugged at her sleeve. "Mommy, we're late. Grant is waiting for us. Can't you do that in the car?"

Rebecca considered the suggestion. But she didn't want to be fixing her hair in the car in front of Grant. It made her feel too self-conscious. She glanced at her watch. They *were* late. "I'll just wear it down," she said finally. She tossed the pins on her dresser and whisked a brush through her hair.

"That looks good," Nora said, standing behind her. "You don't have to wear it pinned up like Mary Poppins all the time."

"Nora...since when do you think I look like Mary Poppins?" Rebecca replied, feeling genuinely shocked at the comparison.

Nora shrugged. "Not in a bad way...I'm just saying your hair looks nice loose, too."

Mary Poppins, indeed. Rebecca silently bristled. Did she really look like the stuffy British nanny? She hurriedly closed their door, grabbed Nora's hand and walked as briskly as she dared through the big house, to the front door.

Finally, she opened the door and stepped onto the covered portico, feeling breathless and unaccountably nervous. It was silly really. She knew Grant so well, yet she felt as jumpy as if she were in high school, going on her first date. At least she had on a new outfit, a form-fitting wheat-colored linen sheath and matching three-quarter-length jacket, worn with a pearl necklace and small gold earrings. Nothing Mary Poppins about it, either, she assured herself.

The first thing she saw was the long, white limousine. She knew Grant owned several cars, one to suit each mood, it seemed, including a sleek black Jaguar and a sturdy metallic gray Land Rover. But she'd never seen the limo.

"Wow, we're going to ride in *that?* Awesome!" Nora exclaimed. She raced toward the car, and the uniformed driver opened the door for her. Then Rebecca caught sight of Grant, who had been standing on the other side of the car.

"There you are. I was starting to get worried that you'd stood me up."

He greeted her with a smile, his white teeth flashing against his richly tanned skin. He was dressed in a charcoal gray suit with a pale pinstripe, along with a white shirt and patterned burgundy silk tie. He looked so handsome, her breath caught in her throat.

"We had a little...delay," Rebecca explained, not wishing to admit she'd been fussing with her hair. "Nothing important," she added.

He'd come around the car and stood facing her. He seemed very tall today, tall and imposing, towering over her. Maybe it was the suit, she told herself. Or his confident attitude. Or the way his dark gaze moved over her, appraising her appearance.

"Let's get going then, shall we? We have an early reservation for lunch, and we'll be cutting it quite close as it is."

"Yes, of course," she agreed. Yet she still didn't move.

"Why are you staring at me?"

"Was I?" She felt herself flush. "Sorry...I didn't mean to. You just look different today," she admitted.

"It must be the suit," he said.

"No, I don't think so," she replied, still staring but unable to help herself. "It's something else." She met his puzzled gaze, then realized what it was. "Your hair. You had it cut."

"Yes, I had a haircut. Don't I always?" he asked defensively.

His surly tone made Rebecca smile. It brought back memories of their early days together. As far as she could see, it was only Joe who chopped into his hair every few weeks, when it got so shaggy not even Grant could stand it anymore. But she held her tongue, knowing he already felt self-conscious under her scrutiny.

"Well, maybe you've found a new barber then. It looks very nice like that," she added gently. "Shows off your handsome face."

She saw a smile tugging at the corner of his mouth. He was pleased with her compliment. Very pleased.

"Thank you, Rebecca," he said smoothly. His dark gaze swept her body, taking in every inch of her. "You look pretty wonderful yourself, if you don't mind me saying so."

She smiled, feeling warmed from head to toe. "I don't mind at all," she admitted. Hoping the shadows in the car would hide her blush, she ducked her head and got in.

The drive to the city passed very quickly. Nora had seen plenty of limousines before but had never been inside one, and she occupied most of Grant's time asking for demonstrations of all the gadgetry. To his credit, Rebecca noticed, he had unlimited patience with her curiosity and seemed to enjoy letting her use the phone, the notebook computer, stereo system and TV—complete with a VCR, of course. Not to mention the minibar, where Nora found many drinks and snacks suited perfectly to her taste.

"Do you always stock your car with Yoohoo?" Rebecca asked him in an amused tone.

"Always," he answered with a shrug. "I keep it right next to the Dom Perignon." His quick comeback made her laugh.

At the Plaza Hotel, they were showered with star treatment from the moment they arrived. Although a line of guests waited for tables in the Palm Court, they were ushered through the crowd and seated in a choice location. It was a beautiful setting, with the fabulous palms and sumptuous decor. Two musicians in formal attire played classical pieces on a violin and cello. Rebecca felt as if she'd been transported to another world. The look on Nora's face expressed the same feeling, only more so.

Grant had thought of everything—he'd even brought along a slim automatic camera to take pictures. Rebecca thought it looked awfully expensive and delicate, and she shuddered when Grant offered Nora a chance to take a few shots. But it was obviously simple to use and a perfect amusement for Nora while they waited for their lunch. She was thrilled to take photos of everything she saw, including Grant and Rebecca.

"You're sitting too far apart," her little voice insisted as she gazed at them through the shutter.

"How's this?" Grant asked. He leaned over and swiftly drew Rebecca to him in a close embrace. For the blink of an eye, Rebecca savored the heat of his nearness.

"Perfect," Nora said, snapping the photo. Rebecca turned to see Grant wearing a wide grin. She was sure her expression in the photo would be one of pure shock.

"That could be a good one, Nora. I can't wait to see it," he joked as he took the camera.

Before Rebecca could comment, the waiter arrived with their lunch. The food was as splendid as the setting, and just when Rebecca thought she couldn't eat another bite, the waiter appeared with a birthday cake decorated with a sparkler and real miniature orchids and satin ribbons. The other waiters gathered around and sang a rousing round of "Happy Birthday."

Nora squeezed her eyes shut and blew out the candles in one breath as Grant captured the moment on film. Everyone in the restaurant applauded, and Nora looked totally pleased. Rebecca could only imagine what she had wished for.

Rebecca had given Nora her presents that morning, a new watch, some clothes she'd asked for and a book by her favorite author. Nora had seemed very pleased by the gifts, and Rebecca knew she didn't expect more. Now Rebecca wondered if she should have saved at least one box to open after the cake. She was sorry she hadn't thought of it.

"Chocolate, my favorite," Nora said as she took a huge bite of cake. "How did you know?"

"Lucky guess," Grant teased with a grin. "I almost forgot." He leaned over and pulled a slim box from his pocket. "Here's a little present for you. Happy birthday, Nora."

A present? And it looked like jewelry, no less. Rebecca couldn't quite believe he'd gone and got Nora an expensive present on top of everything else. It was just too much.

"Thank you, Grant," Nora said sweetly, as she eagerly undid the wrapping. She opened the box and peered inside. "Wow...a real gold locket. Look, Mommy," she exclaimed, holding her gift for Rebecca to see.

"It's beautiful, Nora," Rebecca said honestly. She glanced at Grant. "It is lovely, Grant. You shouldn't have gone to such trouble, though."

"It was no trouble." He sat beaming at Nora, clearly pleased his choice had been a hit. "Here, let me help you put it on," he offered.

Nora came around to his side of the table, and Grant fastened it for her. "It opens up, you know, to put pictures inside."

"Does it really?" She quickly figured out how to open it, and did so. Rebecca watched her look inside the locket, then saw her sudden wide grin. "Grant, you're so silly," Nora said to him.

They were both laughing, and Rebecca felt left out of the joke. "What's so funny?" she asked.

"Look, Mommy." Nora turned the locket so Rebecca could see. "Grant put a picture of Eloise in here for me. Isn't that silly?"

Rebecca didn't know why, but the simple gesture was very touching. Jack had never given—or even mailed—Nora such a lovely, thoughtful gift. She felt her eyes glaze over then forced herself to be bright.

"Yes, very silly," she agreed. She turned to Grant and smiled at him, then reached across the table and took his hand in hers. "You really can be awfully silly sometimes," she told him.

"Yes, I know...in addition to all my other shortcomings, of course,'' he admitted with a sly, sexy grin as he returned the pressure of her touch. "How long can you put up with me, Rebecca?" he asked cryptically.

"As long as you need me, I guess," she answered quietly, unable to break her gaze from his.

It was Nora's excited voice that broke the spell, drawing them back to reality. "We didn't see the portrait of Eloise yet," she said. "Can we go look for it now?"

"Of course," Grant said. "That's a great idea."

Rebecca was about to help him from his chair, but in the blink of an eye, he was standing up, discreetly aided by the use of his cane, and helping her out of her seat in a very gentlemanly fashion.

It took Rebecca a moment to orient herself to the role reversal. She felt him pull back her chair, and she rose smoothly and smiled. "Thank you," she said, meeting his eye.

"Not at all," he replied with a small smile. "Shall we?" he asked, gesturing for her to go before him.

After lunch, they visited the zoo in Central Park and took a carriage ride. There was shopping on Fifth Avenue, where Grant insisted on buying Nora the largest stuffed dog Rebecca had ever seen. When they found it was too large to fit in the trunk of the limousine, Grant had it sent to Bridgehampton that very day so Nora would have it when she got home.

As they strolled down the avenue past Tiffany's, Grant pointed out a pair of breathtaking emerald earrings displayed in the window.

"Emeralds would be perfect for you," he remarked, as if suddenly inspired. "When is your birthday, anyway, Rebecca?"

Rebecca turned to him, not knowing what to say. Did he really think he would buy her emerald earrings for a birthday gift? No, he had to be teasing, she reasoned.

"Oh, too bad," she said lightly. "My birthday's in June. You missed it."

"That was a well-kept secret, wasn't it?" he asked, meeting her gaze. "There's always Christmas. I'll make it up to you then," he added, his tone halfway between a threat and a promise.

She knew he had to be teasing her. By Christmas he'd be so immersed in his real life, she was sure he'd barely recall her name.

They reached the car, and she was saved from continuing the silly conversation. The rest of the day was a blur of activity, with Nora and Grant calling all the shots. Although she'd raised Nora in Manhattan, Rebecca rarely had the time or money to take Nora around the city in such a fashion. Of course, on rainy days she'd drag Nora through a museum or two, and once she took her to the top of the Empire State Building. But their outings had been nothing like this one.

Rebecca enjoyed seeing the city as a tourist would, and she was happy to sit back and take orders for once—though she did grit her teeth and squeeze Grant's fingers until he yelped with pain during the helicopter ride.

After an early dinner at a beautiful restaurant on the East River, Rebecca expected they'd return home.

But Grant had one more surprise up his sleeve—orchestra seats to a Broadway show Nora had been longing to see.

Nora jumped out of her seat with excitement when Grant made the announcement.

"How did you know she wanted to see that show?" Rebecca asked, totally surprised by his choice.

"I make it my business to know these things, Rebecca," he replied, sounding serious, but pleased that she was impressed.

Yes, he had made it his business to please Nora today, Rebecca had to admit. To please both of them, she added silently. His efforts made her love him even more. Which was a good thing and a bad thing. She silently pondered as she gazed out the restaurant window at the river view and the twinkling lights on the opposite shore.

Nora sat attentive and alert through the entire show, and Rebecca enjoyed watching her take it all in. After the show, they had barely driven a block in the car when Rebecca felt her daughter cuddle against her and rest her head in Rebecca's lap. Within seconds, Nora was deeply asleep.

"She's out like a light," she whispered to Grant. "I don't know how I'll ever get her up tomorrow for the camping trip."

Grant glanced at Nora, who sat between them, with a soft smile. "Don't worry. She'll get up. She'll be excited all over again about the camping."

Rebecca had to agree. She could see that he was able to predict Nora's moods and reactions almost as well as she did. With Nora asleep, the ride to Bridge-hampton was very quiet. Grant barely spoke, and Rebecca wondered if all the activity had been taxing for him, too. Perhaps he was in some pain but too macho to admit it. Despite all the time they'd spent together in the past weeks, for some reason Rebecca felt very tense in his presence tonight. Maybe it was the darkness, and the enclosed atmosphere of the car. She glanced at him. He was staring straight ahead. She wondered if he'd fallen asleep, as well.

"Grant?" she whispered quietly. He quickly turned to look at her, and she knew he hadn't been sleeping. "I just want to thank you for today. Nora was thrilled. It was wonderful. You went to far too much trouble, though. It was too generous of you."

"Nonsense," he replied curtly, looking straight ahead again. "It was a selfish gesture on my part, actually. I don't have anyone special in my life to please, Rebecca. I don't have anyone to surprise with a birthday cake or a helicopter ride. Watching the look on her face all day, and yours," he added, "was a rare pleasure for me. So maybe I should be the one thanking you."

"You're welcome," she replied. "Very welcome. You would always be," she added quietly. He met her gaze, and even in the car's dark shadows, she could see the intense emotion in his expression.

He reached over the back of the seat and slipped his arm around her shoulder with Nora cuddled between them. She welcomed his touch and dropped her head to his shoulder.

As they drove in silence, Rebecca felt his quiet

words deep in her heart. Underneath it all, he was a
lonely man, trapped in a prison of his own making.
He could reach out to her this way. With his tender
insights, he could almost tempt her into believing
there was a real future for them. But finally, what
would it all add up to? A broken heart for her, she
knew for sure. And maybe even for him, as well.

When they arrived at the house, Rebecca was surprised to realize she'd fallen asleep on Grant's shoulder. "We're home," he whispered in her ear without
stirring a muscle.

She turned her head to find his face just inches
away. "Oh, dear. I fell asleep on you. Sorry."

He smiled. "Don't be." He cupped her cheek in
his hand and dropped a sweet, lingering kiss on her
mouth. Rebecca sleepily kissed him back, feeling so
warm and relaxed, the kiss could have lasted forever.

Finally, with a reluctant sigh, he withdrew from her
and whispered, "Better wake up Nora."

"Yes," she agreed as they slowly broke apart. She
had to wake up and stop dreaming, as well.

Eight

As Rebecca had predicted, it was tough going the next morning, getting Nora out of the house and to her camp bus by seven-thirty. She felt a bit teary, waving to Nora as the bus pulled away. It was only a weekend, she reminded herself. But Rebecca knew she'd miss Nora's bright, sprightly company.

Rebecca had coffee and a roll at a café in town, then did some errands. She returned to the Berringer estate just before noon feeling tired and tempted to take a nap, an indulgence she rarely allowed herself.

The note taped to her door had the effect of a double espresso, jolting her out of her lethargy. She could see right away it was written in Grant's handwriting, and the simple message inside made her heart race. "Had a great catch this morning. And won't have to throw it back this time. Have dinner with me? Grant."

Rebecca leaned against her closed door. The silence of her rooms, a subtle reminder of Nora's absence, and the note in her hand caused reality to sink in. She was alone in the house with Grant. Utterly alone until Sunday night when Nora returned. Even Mrs. Walker had been given the weekend off to visit her grandchildren in Massachusetts.

Whenever Rebecca had considered this situation, she'd assured herself it was a very large house and that she could easily avoid Grant for two days, even more if she needed to.

But did she want to? That was the real question. She dropped onto the sofa and looked at the note again. She recalled the way he'd kissed her last night when they'd arrived home. He was the one who had pulled away. She had not wanted the kiss to end.

Yesterday, he'd given Nora a day to remember for all time. But while the memories were sweet, Rebecca knew what she and Grant could share together, intimately, as a man and a woman, would be a thrill far beyond that of a helicopter ride. A ride in the space shuttle might not even compare. She quietly smiled.

To accept his invitation to dinner would be, in her mind, a tacit agreement to spend the night with him. For she knew very well that's what this invitation was all about. If she refused, he'd be a gentleman, she was sure, and would leave her alone for the rest of the weekend.

She strolled to the glass doors that led to the deck. What did she want, she asked herself. The answer was simple. As simple as the sight of the brilliantly shining sun and rolling blue sea. She wanted him. She wanted to know what it was like to love him and feel his love in return. To join with him, be part of him. Maybe it tarnished her professional standards. Maybe it was a hopeless gesture, a tantalizing taste of a future that could never be.

But that's what she wanted. And by heaven, Rebecca knew, down deep in the pit of her soul, she would not—and could not—deny herself this experience. It would hurt later. Hurt plenty, she had no doubt. But when she looked back on the choice, years and years from now, it would be one she knew she'd never regret.

Before reason and secret fears could change her mind, Rebecca picked up the phone and dialed Grant's extension. He picked up on one ring, and before he had time to say hello, she accepted his dinner invitation in an embarrassed rush of words.

"Great," he replied, sounding genuinely pleased. He accepted Rebecca's offer to help fix the meal. "I warn you, I'm a tyrant in the kitchen. Worse than you are in the workout room."

"We'll see who's worse," she replied, smiling.

Rebecca found she was smiling after she hung up the phone, and still smiling when she strolled to the beach, took a swim and then napped in the sun. She was smiling the entire day, in fact, in anticipation of the night ahead.

Rebecca dressed casually, in a short, slip-style sundress with a peach background and a print of scattered flowers. An armful of silver bracelets and small silver earrings gave the dress a more high-fashion touch, as did her sleek long ponytail. She felt relaxed from her leisurely afternoon on the beach, and her fair complexion looked golden and glowing. For makeup, she needed only a dash of mascara, lip gloss and a brief touch of her favorite perfume at her wrists and nape.

She entered the kitchen and found Grant standing at the counter, chopping something on a wooden block. He turned and took her in with a long, sweeping stare, then let out a long, low whistle.

"If I knew you were going to look that gorgeous, Rebecca, I would have taken you out, just to show you off," he admitted.

Rebecca pursed her lips but couldn't hide her blush. "Thanks for the compliment," she replied. "Even though that's a perfectly chauvinistic thing to say," she added with a laugh.

"Now, now," he reprimanded her. "Would a true chauvinist be standing here up to his elbows in chopped parsley...wearing an apron, no less?"

With her hands on her hips and her head cocked, she looked him over. He looked pretty darned cute in his apron, she had to admit.

"No, I guess not," she agreed. She walked to him. "What can I do to help, boss?" she asked with a twinkle in her eye.

"First, pour yourself a glass of wine," he instructed, pointing out the wine bottle and glass. "Then you can help me chop up these herbs."

They worked together companionably, preparing the fish and other dishes. Grant was terribly bossy, scolding her about the way she chopped or carried out some other task. But Rebecca managed to laugh at him and patiently followed his exacting instructions.

They ate on the terrace, an array of glimmering candles on the table and glittering stars above. The fresh-grilled fish had a subtle but superb flavor, and Rebecca was lavish with her compliments to the chef.

"It was nothing," he said modestly. "Just some herbs and lemon butter. It's hard to ruin a nice fresh fish like this one. Although I do have to take some credit for catching it."

"Yes, you do," Rebecca agreed. "And I won't mention a word to Nora, if you don't," she added.

"Heaven forbid," he replied. He took a sip of his wine. "She might decide that it was the same fish she'd set free."

Rebecca paused, a forkful of food midway between the plate and her mouth. "It wasn't, of course...was it?" she asked quietly.

Grant met her gaze and laughed. "Of course not. That fish was too smart to come back in this direction."

They talked easily through the meal about varied and wide-ranging topics. Rebecca loved to talk with Grant. He knew so much about so many things. He had traveled all over the world and had packed so much experience into his life so far. Yet he listened quietly and seriously when she offered her opinions. His mind was quick, his wit sharp and irreverent. Although she often disagreed with him, their conversation was never boring.

Grant served coffee, and they both decided they were too full for dessert—a fabulous chocolate mousse that had been delivered from a gourmet shop in town. Rebecca sipped her coffee and felt a tense silence fall between them. She found herself toying with her napkin, then felt Grant's touch on her hand, stilling her fingertips.

"You know, I've really come a long way in my therapy these past few weeks, Rebecca. I can walk on my own, swim, fish, even cook dinner."

"Yes, you're doing very well," Rebecca agreed, wondering where the conversation was leading. "Exceptionally well," she added. Was he about to say, in a polite way, that he no longer needed her services?

"There is one thing I really wanted to try tonight," he said in a quiet, seductive tone. "Something I haven't been able to do for a long, long time," he added, with longing underscoring every word.

"Oh…and what's that?" she asked breathlessly. She felt his hand on her shoulder, adjusting the thin strap on her dress. She swallowed hard but didn't dare look at him.

"I'd like to dance with you," he said simply. "Will you dance with me, Rebecca?"

She met his gaze and caught the teasing light in his dark eyes. He knew he had scared her. On purpose, too. She felt a smile tugging at the corners of her lips, but held it back.

"Yes, Grant. I'd love to dance with you," she said. She waited until he rose and helped her from her chair. Then she turned and moved smoothly into his open arms. The first contact of his hard, warm body on hers was heavenly, and Rebecca realized she'd been secretly waiting for this moment the entire evening.

His arms circled her waist, and he pulled her close. She needed little coaxing to tuck her head against his shoulder. Grant had chosen some jazz CDs for their dinner music, and the song that played was a sultry jazz ballad. Their bodies swayed together in time to the beat. Grant's step was slow but steady. Her arms circled his muscular shoulders, her fingers moving into his dark hair as she breathed in the familiar scent of him, his warm skin and spicy cologne. She felt totally intoxicated. Her head spun from his nearness, his firm, muscular body moving against her own, the magic of the sultry music and her powerful longing.

When she felt his mouth moving against the skin of her bare shoulder, her head dropped to the side, giving him freer access to the smooth column of her neck.

"Hmm, you taste delicious. I wish I could have you for dessert," he murmured playfully as his hands moved firmly over her back and hips, molding her slim form. "May I?" he asked, in a husky, sexy whisper.

Rebecca turned her head, seeking and finding his mouth with hers. She tilted her head to kiss him fully, conveying the desire she felt more clearly than words could.

Finally, she pulled away, meeting his startled gaze with hers. "Yes," she said simply.

It took an instant for her meaning to register. Rebecca watched as his expression quickly turned from surprise to happiness to intense, ignited desire.

She felt his grip on her body tighten as he pressed her closer. His arousal at her nearness was plainly evident. It excited her.

"I could make love to you right here, on that lounge chair," he admitted in a low growl close to her ear, "but I won't. This is going to be perfect for you."

She pulled back and stared into his eyes as she lovingly touched his face with her hand. Her fingertips traced the hard line of his cheek to his jaw, grazing the slight ridge of his scar. "If I'm in your arms," she answered finally, "I can't imagine how it could be anything less."

He gazed at her. About to say something, she thought. And yet, no words came. Finally, his head dipped to the lure of her moist, red lips. Their mouths met and merged, his kiss questioning at first. Then, as he felt her eager response, the kiss quickly deepened to a passionate expression of Grant's deep need for her. And her need for him.

Finally, he drew away from her, his hands sliding up to cup her bare shoulders. He pressed his cheek against her hair, catching his breath and inhaling her flowery scent. "Come with me to my room," he whispered. Rebecca nodded in answer, too overwhelmed to speak.

Grant wrapped his arm around her waist and dropped a kiss on her hair as she fell into step with him. Rebecca was thankful his rooms were only a short walk from the terrace. Her legs felt so weak and rubbery, she wasn't sure she could make it very far. Within moments they arrived and went inside. Rebecca heard Grant close the door behind them and was glad to find there were no lights. The curtains were open, and light from the full moon that had risen over the sea bathed the room in a silvery glow.

When Rebecca turned toward him, she could discern only his tall outline. But then he came closer, and her heart pounded wildly. He stepped toward her and cupped her bare shoulders in his hands. He pressed his cheek against her hair, breathing in the rich scent of her hair and skin.

Rebecca moved smoothly into his embrace, her arms looping around his waist, her soft, full breasts pressed to his chest. She stirred against him, murmured his name, and his arms moved to encircle her, gripping her tightly to him. His hands immediately moved to her hair and unfastened the clip that held it back.

"You make me feel so alive, Rebecca. You brought me back to life, you know. But even better this time than before," he murmured as he dug his fingers into her hair and spread it across her shoulders. "Before I met you, even before the accident, I never felt quite this way. So awake, so aware. So eager for every sensation. You've done that to me," he confessed as he dropped soft kisses on her shoulders, then followed the soft curve of her neck. She sighed, unable to answer him, unable to think.

He lifted her face to his. His eyes looked huge and bright, dark as the sea and churning with a passion that both thrilled and terrified her. She ran her hands along the hard planes of his back and tipped her head, unable to pull her gaze from his. He made her feel

alive, too. Full of life and eager to love him completely. She didn't have to say it. She was sure he
could see it in her eyes, feel it in her touch, taste it
in her kiss.

Finally, their mouths met and merged. Her hands
glided over his muscular chest and shoulders, then to
his back again, boldly caressing him. Grant answered
her touch with a sweep of his large warm hands down
the curves of her lithe form, from her shoulders to
her hips, then up again, to gently cup her full breasts.
Rebecca didn't realize when he slipped down the thin
straps of her dress, but soon she was bare to the waist
except for her lacy, strapless bra. Grant's warm mouth
pressed against the soft curves of her breasts, his fingertips circling the hardened tips. The material of her
dress felt like airy thin gauze that floated down her
hips and pooled at her feet as he touched and caressed
her. Her kiss was wild against his mouth for a moment before she softly moaned with pleasure, her
body sagging helplessly against him. She felt his hand
press against her flat stomach, his fingertips grazing
the edge of her bikini underwear.

"You're so beautiful," he whispered in a husky
voice. "You take my breath away."

Moments later, they dropped onto his bed. As their
kisses grew wilder and more intense, Grant cushioned
Rebecca's head with one strong arm, the other stroking her from hip to thigh. His mouth moved from her
lips, down the smooth column of her throat and across
the silky skin at the edge of her bra. With his fingertips and tongue he teased and tasted the soft, sensitive
flesh at the top of her cleavage and removed the scrap

of lace entirely, exposing her breasts to his passionate
touch.

Rebecca's fingers moved restlessly through his
thick hair as his mouth covered one rosy, sensitive
nipple. She moaned and stirred under him, pressing
her hips provocatively against his. She felt his read-
iness for her, his throbbing need to make them one.
She heard him take a deep, ragged breath as he lifted
his head and looked at her.

Her eyes were half-closed, dazed with passion, her
face flushed, her glorious red hair splayed around her
head.

"Rebecca," he whispered. He kissed her lightly
and then swallowed hard. "If you want me to stop, I
will," he whispered hoarsely. "I just want you to be
sure."

She framed his face with her cool, soft hands and
looked deeply into his eyes. "I've never been surer
of anything in my life," she promised him.

He didn't answer, but in the tense set of his jaw
she saw a small pulse beating madly out of control.
She ran her hands along the sculpted planes of his
back again, then slipped her hands under his shirt and
pulled open the buttons. Her touch clearly thrilled
him, and Rebecca felt her confidence to satisfy him
grow. She pressed her mouth to his chest, kissing him,
tasting him, her warm, wet tongue swirling around
his sensitive flat nipples. She felt his body shudder
and heard him moan with pleasure as her caresses
moved lower, her mouth tenderly exploring his flat
abdomen, her hands caressing his chest and then his
thighs. She unfastened his belt and the top of his

pants, then slipped her hand inside his pants to cup and caress his male hardness, stroking him until he groaned and grasped her hard, responding to the intense pleasure of her touch.

Finally, pulling back from her seductive caresses, Grant raised himself above her, his hand sliding up her smooth, strong leg. His fingertips found the lacy edge of her panties and his fingers slipped inside, seeking and finding her slick velvety warmth. Her hips arched into his touch, and she knew he could feel that she was ready for him, more than ready.

As she shifted restlessly against him, Grant stilled her with a long, lingering kiss. ''Not so fast, sweetheart. I told you before, I want to make this perfect for you.''

Rebecca clung to him and felt herself drowning in wave after wave of pleasure while his fingers expertly stroked the peak of her pulsing womanhood. He was the most sensitive and masterful lover she'd ever known, alert to the slightest shift of her body, the slightest change in her breath, eager to please her, to touch her exactly as she wanted. His mouth moved again to her breasts, sucking and soothing her nipples. Rebecca sighed and writhed with pleasure as his expert loving pushed her higher and higher. She gripped his powerful shoulders, her hips thrusting to meet the lovingly slow strokes of his hand.

Finally, she couldn't bear it anymore. She trembled and moaned and pressed her face into the hollow between his neck and shoulder. She took a deep, shuddering breath and pressed herself close to him.

"Was that good?" he asked quietly, kissing her hair.

"Unbearably good...and it can only get better," she added in a sultry whisper. "Come to me," she urged him. With her hands on his hips, she gently guided his body to cover hers. "I want you so badly," she confessed.

"I want you more," he whispered. "I never wanted a woman more than I want you...or waited longer to have her."

Then his mouth pressed passionately to hers, and he shifted his body and settled between her thighs. Moments later, he made their bodies one.

Rebecca drew in a sharp and ragged breath. Her body tensed, then trembled in his arms. He held very still, kissing her hair until he felt her relax beneath him. Then he began to move slowly inside her, and she moaned deep and low at the back of her throat. The sound of pure, uninhibited pleasure seemed to thrill him, inspiring him to move deeper, to give her even more.

Their bodies moved as one in an ageless rhythm, an echo of the steady pounding of the waves against the shoreline just beyond their door. Grant thrust faster and deeper as Rebecca met him sigh for sigh, rising to meet him, driving him wild with passion.

He was indescribably beautiful, powerful, unique and precious to her. Rebecca knew suddenly that she had never loved anyone more, and never would again, no matter how long she lived. As he brought her to a climax of pleasure and she felt him reaching his own, in some dim, distant part of her heart, she knew that this session of lovemaking had not served to satisfy one single drop of her longing for him. To the contrary, to hold him and love him this way had given her a taste of what could be and an everlasting longing that would never be satisfied.

Just as she felt herself reaching the peak, she heard Grant's cries of ecstasy and felt him shudder in her arms. Their mouths merged in a deep, devouring kiss as Grant moved within her with one last, powerful thrust. She shivered and gripped him close, calling his name as her body clenched around him, and they cleaved together as one, as close as two beings could ever be.

Rebecca lay with her eyes closed, unwilling to come down off her lovely cloud of bliss. She felt limp and spent, her body still tingling with tiny lights, like the last embers of fireworks left sparkling in the sky.

Grant remained on top of her. When he made a move to shift away, she held him fast. "No...not yet. I like the way you feel on top of me," she whispered.

He lifted his head, and she saw the flash of his smile in the darkness. "You're an angel, Rebecca," he whispered. He dropped soft kisses on her forehead, cheek and chin. "An angel to make love with, that's for sure," he added. He pressed his cheek to hers and sighed. "Will you stay here with me tonight, the whole night, I mean? I want to wake up next to you."

What a lovely idea, she thought. She smiled at him. "Well, you've already seen me first thing in the morning, so that part won't be any surprise."

"You look beautiful no matter when I see you," he replied. "You always take my breath away."

She blushed, unable to believe his compliment. "You don't have to tell me things like that, Grant. I don't need...outrageous compliments."

He shifted to his side and rested his head on his hand. "It's only the simple truth, Rebecca. Even looking at you right now, I want you all over again." He reached out and gently brushed a strand of hair off her bare breast, his fingertips lingering on her silky skin, teasing her until she felt her nipple harden, though he never touched her there. "Even more than before, if that's possible."

Staring deeply into her eyes, he pulled her long leg up to cover his hip, and she felt the hard evidence of his renewed desire. His hand covered her breast and his mouth sought hers again, his slow, deep kisses kindling her deepest fires.

Rebecca would have never guessed that she could be ready to make love again so quickly. But she was. And with tender touches and even more imaginative ways of pleasuring him, she showed Grant how much she wanted him, too.

Rebecca woke up the next morning in Grant's arms. At first she felt confused and disoriented. Then memories of their night together flooded back with amazing clarity. She realized she was naked under the sheet, and so was Grant. His warm, hair-covered body was curled next to hers, as intimately as two could be. She liked the feeling of his heavy arm draped across her waist. She held perfectly still, trying not to wake him. She wanted to enjoy the moment before he woke and pulled away.

She glanced at the clock on the night table and noticed that they had slept late. It was nearly nine. She also noticed that the large framed photo of Courtney was gone. Grant had put it someplace else or put it away altogether. She hadn't given the photo—or his lost fiancée—a thought last night. Everything had been so perfect between them, so passionate and loving. She didn't allow her mind to entertain a single thought or insecurity that would have spoiled it.

But now she wondered if Grant's feelings about the past had changed since they'd last spoken about his accident and unhappy memories. Clearly, he seemed happier, eager to embrace life and move forward with his recovery. Did that mean he saw a future for them? They'd made love endlessly, and he'd praised her and complimented her to the stars. Yet he'd never once mentioned the word love or anything close to it. Well, it was far too soon for that, Rebecca thought. She felt grateful for the precious hours she'd spent in his arms. Maybe that was all she would ever have with him, she realized, the sum total of their entire affair. But she knew that going in, she reminded herself. If that's all he could give her, she'd have no regrets. Certainly, compared to the alternative—having no chance to share her love with him—she'd take it. She turned her face on the pillow and watched him sleep. He was so handsome, so utterly masculine looking with his tanned skin, dark bearded cheeks and sleep-tousled hair. He'd been hers alone, at least for one night. In her heart, she knew she'd always belong to him.

She had no idea what the future would hold for them, and Rebecca was determined not to break the

fragile spell they'd woven last night with her inse-
curities.

Grant slowly opened his eyes to find her staring at
him. She smiled, and he smiled back. "I got my
wish," he said quietly. "There you are, the first thing
I see."

"Here I am," Rebecca greeted him. She touched
his cheek with her hand. "It's late, after nine."

His smile grew wider. "We were tired...under-
standably so." His hand skimmed the bare skin of her
hip, moving down to her slim thigh. "I'll make us
some breakfast," he offered. "How about pancakes?"

"Good, I'm hungry."

"I'm hungry, too," he replied, his gaze fixed on
hers. "Hungry for you again," he added before moving closer for a kiss.

Rebecca opened her arms to him and held him
close as he kissed her and kissed her again. As she
felt her body awaken to his touch, she realized she
could happily wait for her pancakes. If necessary, she
could wait all day.

After breakfast, which qualified more as brunch,
Rebecca and Grant decided to go out for the day.
Since Grant was still unable to drive, he persuaded
Rebecca to get behind the wheel of his Saab con-
vertible. Rebecca felt very nervous at first, thinking
she was going to dent the expensive car at every turn.
But she soon grew used to it and began to enjoy the
way the automobile handled so easily.

They drove around the countryside, stopping to
browse antique sheds and the beautiful shops that

lined the streets of the nearby towns, which catered
to the wealthy summer visitors.

Grant wanted to drive to North Fork, which was
considerably quieter, not quite as fashionable and still
full of farms and vineyards. Late in the day, they
stopped at a vineyard for lunch and sampled the fea-
tured wine, an icy cold Pinot Grigio, while a violinist
played a beautiful classical piece, her backdrop the
rolling acres of the vineyard.

Later, as they strolled the streets of the harbor vil-
lage hand in hand, Rebecca felt truly hopeful, as if
all the loose ends had finally come together for them.
Could Grant have overcome the barriers of his past?
She wanted so much to speak to him about it, but
knew it was best to wait for him to say something. It
was a struggle, but somehow Rebecca managed to
hold her tongue, to relax and enjoy the day.

All too soon, it seemed, the sun began to set, and
it was time to pick up Nora. As they drove to the
pickup location in town, Rebecca was suddenly eager
to see her daughter.

"I wonder if she had a good time," Rebecca said,
thinking out loud. "I remember my first sleep away.
I felt a spider crawling over my hand right after
lights-out, and I didn't sleep a wink all night."

Grant laughed. "You poor kid. I'm sure Nora loved
it. Even if she met a spider or two."

"She'll have a lot of stories," Rebecca agreed,
knowing how her daughter loved to report every de-
tail of her outings.

"Yes, she will," Grant said. "I can't wait to hear

them,'' he added, his hand gently stroking her shoulders as she drove.

Nora was elated but exhausted. As Rebecca had guessed, she talked nonstop all the way home. Grant encouraged her to tell all with his questions. After they returned and had all climbed out of the car, Nora turned to Rebecca and Grant and flung her arms around both adults. "I missed you guys," she said, her face muffled in Rebecca's skirt.

Grant rested his hand on Nora's head. "We missed you, too, Nora," he said. "It was very quiet around here. Too quiet."

She looked up and grinned at him. "What did you guys do all weekend? I'll bet it got boring without me."

Rebecca saw a grin on Grant's face, and he briefly met her gaze before looking at Nora. "Not boring. No, I wouldn't say that at all," he replied slowly, choosing his words with care. "Your mom and I managed to...keep busy," he said simply.

Rebecca smiled. That was one way of describing the weekend. She silently laughed.

The following days seemed to mark a new start for them, and Rebecca felt closer than ever to Grant. She didn't fear the end of the summer anymore, but looked ahead with hopeful anticipation. Grant's healing no longer seemed to signify the end of their time together. It seemed to be a step toward a new level in their relationship. It was hard to keep their intimate bond a secret from the household. Grant wanted to shout the news from the rooftops, but Rebecca didn't feel ready to share their secret with the world. The charade made Rebecca feel silly and childish sometimes. Especially at night, when Grant would visit her bed for a few precious hours of passionate lovemaking.

Secrecy was not natural to Rebecca's open nature. But she felt that in this case, it was for the best. She worried about Nora. She knew her daughter would be thrilled to learn that Grant was her mother's official "boyfriend"—but what if it didn't work out? Rebecca knew Nora had suffered enough disappointment over the divorce. She worried that Nora's hopes would be raised by the prospect of having Grant as a stepfather, but she might end up hurt and disappointed again. In the interest of protecting her, Rebecca persuaded Grant to keep their relationship under wraps, at least until they were in the city, living separately and feeling sure about where they were headed.

Sometimes Grant acted very confidently about their future. His casual comments about things they would do and places they'd go, would make her head spin in a happy daze. If it was up to him, it sounded as if they'd never be apart again, as he often hinted about her and Nora moving into his large city apartment at the summer's end. Rebecca had subtly let him know she thought it was too soon for her to think about living together. Especially with Nora involved. She'd been flattered, however, that he wanted such a domestic, permanent arrangement.

Still, she knew it was too early to count on things working out. Grant had never discussed his feelings about the accident. Was he over them? He had never told her point-blank that he loved her, either—though she believed he did, and felt it in his every look, his every kiss, his every loving caress.

They needed time, Rebecca kept telling herself. In time, it might all work out as she dreamed. About two weeks after Nora's camping trip, Grant finished his workout, then surprised Rebecca with a sudden announcement.

"I'm seeing my doctor in the city this week, on Wednesday. I think it's about time I went back to work. What do you say? He'll want your opinion, I'm sure."

Rebecca was startled. She felt blindsided. What did this mean? Was Grant suddenly looking for an easy escape hatch? Was he running to the city to get away from her? She turned, trying to hide her expression, which she was sure would show her distress. She hadn't been the one to pursue him, he'd pursued her. Persuaded her, despite her better judgment, to get involved with him. Was he running from her now? Avoiding a serious commitment?

"Well, what do you think, Rebecca?" he asked curiously. He hopped off the exercise table and followed her. "You seemed concerned. Is there something wrong I should know about?"

"No, not at all," she replied with a brief shake of her head. "You're probably ready to return to work, if you wish. Though you will need to keep up your exercise routine. I just didn't know you were so eager to go back to the city."

"Restless, I guess. I feel so much better lately, I need to do something more productive with my time.'' He lifted her chin with his fingertips and stared at her face. ''I'm not eager to leave you, if that's what you're worried about. Just the opposite, I'd say.''

''I never said I thought that.''

''No…but you didn't have to say it. I know you too well by now, sweetheart,'' he replied. He took her shoulders in his hands, then leaned over and kissed her hard on the mouth. ''I'm better now, finally. I can feel it,'' he told her. ''But it's not the end for us, Rebecca. It's only the beginning,'' he promised.

''Is it?'' she asked him, unable to hide her fears any longer.

He stared at her, then pulled her close in a sheltering embrace. ''Rebecca, please,'' he said, sounding shocked that she even dared to ask such a question. ''I didn't have a future until I met you. And now I couldn't imagine the future without you. You and Nora. I thought you knew that by now.''

''No, I guess I didn't,'' she admitted. She shook her head against his shoulder and felt him softly touch her hair. She felt tears in her eyes. She didn't want him to see her cry.

''I know you have your work, but we'll be together, won't we?'' he asked quietly. ''I mean, you aren't planning to take some new assignment in California or something?''

He was worried about losing her, too. She could hear it in his voice. And all the while, she thought she was the only one who yearned for assurances. Though he still hadn't said he loved her, Rebecca felt she'd heard as much of a promise as she needed. More than she needed to pledge herself to him.

"Don't worry, I can find an assignment in the city," she said simply, winding her arms around his waist. "You won't be getting rid of me that easily."

"Good," he replied, sounding satisfied. He hugged her close. "I won't lose you, Rebecca. Not after we've come this far."

She didn't say a word in reply. She didn't need to. Her heart felt so full of love for him, she thought it might burst. Her answering embrace was more eloquent than words. They *had* come far, she realized. With any luck, one step at a time, they'd make it all the way.

Grant returned from his visit to the city looking haggard and drawn. She worried that the doctor had given him distressing news, or not the news he'd hoped to hear.

But when she tried to draw him out over dinner, his answers were brusque, and even rude. His gruffness hurt her feelings, but Rebecca tried to act as if nothing was the matter. He was retreating into his old, dark mood, she realized, as if he was being pulled away from her by some unseen force. And there was nothing she could do about it.

That night, after Nora had fallen asleep, she went to his room. She knocked quietly, and he came to the door, seeming pleased to see her at first. But after she walked in and closed the door, he turned his back to her, and she heard him sigh.

"Grant, what's the matter? I know something is bothering you." She walked up behind him and rested her hands on his shoulders. "Please talk to me."

"There is something on my mind," he admitted. He glanced at her over his shoulder, then looked away again. "Something troubling. But it's none of your concern, Rebecca," he assured her.

She moved away from him and sat on the edge of his bed. "Please don't say it doesn't concern me. Don't you see? If it troubles you, it troubles me. If you can't be open with me about your problems, Grant, we don't really stand much of a chance."

He turned and gazed at her. She could see his expression softening a bit, though he still looked distant and grim.

"I want a chance with you, Rebecca. I want to have a life with you. I want to watch Nora grow up and have more children with you, too. I want us to grow old together, and stay together forever. I want that more than anything I ever wanted in this world. You believe me when I say that, don't you?" he asked solemnly.

"Yes. Yes, I do." That was exactly what she wanted, too. But his serious expression and tone scared her. She wished he would tell her what was happening. It had to be something bad. Something that threatened their future. She felt it in her bones.

He took a manila folder off his desk and handed it to her. "Here, look at this. These documents were received this morning by special messenger."

She opened the folder and saw some legal documents. She didn't quite know what she was reading but could discern that the form had to do with a lawsuit. It appeared that someone was suing Grant. As far as she could see, it was Courtney's family.

"You're being sued by Courtney's family," she said slowly looking at him.

"That's right. Wrongful death, they're calling it." He took the folder and took a deep anguished breath.

"But whatever for?" she asked, feeling a hollow place open in the pit of her stomach.

"They say it was all my fault, as the driver of the car," he said bitterly, staring at her. "The nightmare just never ends for me, Rebecca. I think it's going to end. I believe I deserve for it to be over. But it doesn't end. I can't get out from under. I can't escape this dark place. It will just keep pulling me back in, again and again."

Rebecca rose and put her arms around him. He dropped his head to her shoulder. She felt his body shake. He was distraught, and like most men, trying to hold it all inside.

She gently pulled him down so they lay on the bed together, then she turned out the light. She held him close and felt him answer her embrace. He soon grew calmer, his breathing even and slow.

"You'll get through this," she promised him, daring finally to speak. "We'll get through it together. It will be okay. You'll see."

He sighed deeply and kissed her hair. But when he finally spoke, Rebecca noticed he'd didn't say that he agreed with her. Instead, he changed the subject completely.

"Stay with me tonight, for a little while," he entreated her. "I want to make love with you. That's all I care about right now. The future will just have to take care of itself somehow."

Without waiting for her reply, he rose over her and pressed his lips to hers. Rebecca wrapped her arms around his strong body and answered his embrace. She was suddenly afraid of the future. Pushing fearful thoughts aside, she willed herself to follow Grant's lead and concentrate on the moment, on the pure and ultimate pleasure of holding the man she loved.

Nine

Several months later, long after Rebecca had left Grant's house in Bridgehampton for a new assignment in Madison, Connecticut, the last words he'd said to her that fateful night continued to prey on her mind. As well as the memories of the last time they made love.

Just as she feared, after he learned of the lawsuit, Grant slipped back to a shadowy place, where memories of the accident and his guilt ruled him. Rebecca's heart broke as she saw him withdraw from her little by little, day by day. She learned that the lawsuit would never go to court. Grant's lawyers were working on a quick settlement. Still, the situation had done its damage, and Rebecca felt her hopes sinking a little more each day, like a ship with a damaged hull.

They began to argue, not the bantering, playful arguments that had always sparked their relationship, but painful, bitter bouts. Rebecca knew that Grant was pushing her away. Time and time again, she wanted to run from him. But she hung on, because she loved him and hoped some miracle would save them.

Finally, one day, he angrily asked her to leave, telling her that her services were no longer required. Rebecca had heard it all before, but this time, the words hit home. Her heart couldn't bear any more pain. And her hope for a miracle had finally run out. She suddenly didn't know how she'd managed to stand it so long. She curtly agreed to his order and went straight to her room and packed.

Nora had been confused about the change in Grant's behavior, but she'd been satisfied by Rebecca's explanation that Grant had a business problem he was trying to work out. To Grant's credit, he was always kind and sweet to Nora, which somehow puzzled the little girl even more.

With tears in her eyes, Rebecca announced that they were leaving the next day. Thankfully, her daughter didn't question her. Rebecca knew she'd never forget the look on Grant's face as he hugged Nora goodbye. She had to look away, there was so much raw emotion there. Their parting was awkward. They stood staring at each other, Rebecca wishing to get through it before she burst into tears.

Grant looked uncomfortable and unhappy, yet relieved, as well, she had thought then. Relieved to be rid of her, relieved to be left alone with his sad, dark memories. She didn't wish to think badly of him—

she never really could. But he had disappointed her. He'd broken her heart as no one ever had before, or ever would again. She would never love any man again as she loved Grant.

She had thought that once they were separated she would gradually forget him, that her feelings would fade, even if she didn't wish it to be so. But she knew that wasn't true. It made no difference if they were together or apart. If she saw him tomorrow or never again. He lived inside her, and her love was an indelible mark on her heart and soul, marking her for him and him alone. She would live the rest of her life missing him as deeply as she missed him that very first day apart.

Her new patient was a ten-year-old boy, Jake Nelson. Jake had fallen out of a tree and broken several bones in his arms and legs. He was determined to play baseball again in the spring, and Rebecca was determined to see him do it.

Rebecca had purposely looked for an assignment near her mother's home, where she and Nora were staying temporarily. She decided not to return to the city for a while. She was not afraid of running into Grant, since New York was such a vast place and they moved in such different circles. But she was afraid of thinking too much of him if they were living in such proximity and thought a change would do her good. Since she'd given up her apartment when she'd started working for Grant, she had no reason to return to the city.

Her mother had guessed that Rebecca was suffering from some romantic disappointment. But she was not the type to pry, for which Rebecca was endlessly grateful. Rebecca did not think she would stay long in her mother's house and was starting to look for a place of her own. But it was the house she'd grown up in and a convenient and comforting resting place for the time being.

Rebecca tried not to think of Grant. But it was an endless battle that didn't get much easier as the weeks passed. As the holidays approached, her thoughts of him grew more intense. She found herself wondering where he'd be and what he'd be doing, remembering that he had so little family.

About a week before Thanksgiving, Rebecca sat with her mother in the kitchen, sipping tea and making a menu for the upcoming family dinner. Both Rebecca's sisters and their families would be arriving next week and staying for the weekend. Rebecca's mother, Alice, was in her usual tizzy, worrying about how she would find everyone a bed and get all the cooking and cleaning done. As Rebecca assured her they'd all pitch in, someone knocked insistently on the front door, and Nora ran to answer it.

"How about the cranberries?" Rebecca asked, trying to get her mother to focus on the menu. "I can make a cranberry relish, with orange and walnuts. It's really good," she promised.

"Sounds perfect," a deep, familiar voice replied.

Rebecca turned, her mouth dropping open. It was Grant. Standing in the doorway of her mother's kitchen, holding Nora's hand. For a moment, she thought she was having a hallucination.

"Look, Mom. Look who came to visit us," Nora

exclaimed happily. Rebecca could see that they had already exchanged greetings.

"My, isn't this a surprise," Rebecca said dryly. He was smiling at her, smiling with his whole heart showing in his eyes, the way he used to do. But it made her sad to look at him, sad and angry. She looked away, into her mug of tea.

"Rebecca?" her mother asked nervously. "Aren't you going to introduce me to your visitor?" she prodded.

Rebecca looked up again, remembering her manners. "Grant, this is my mother, Alice Calloway. Alice, this is Grant Berringer, a former patient."

Did Grant wince at her introduction? If so, he deserved it, she thought.

"It's good to meet you, Mrs. Calloway," Grant said smoothly. He smiled and took her mother's hand.

"Why don't you call me Alice?" Rebecca's mother replied.

Rebecca shook her head. Her mother looked a bit flustered receiving Grant's full attention. She always got that way around a good-looking man.

"And have a seat," Alice urged him, pulling out a chair for Grant to sit in. She glanced from Rebecca to the mysterious stranger. "I have some chores to do upstairs," she added hurriedly. "Nora, you come help me."

"But, Nana..." Nora began.

Alice looked at her over her glasses. "I really need your help, Nora," she insisted. "Upstairs."

Before Rebecca could prevent it, she was left alone

with Grant. He sat close to her, close enough to touch. Though she didn't dare.

"How did you find us?" she asked him.

"It wasn't too hard. I made a few calls. The specialist who first recommended you to my brother knew where you were."

"Oh, of course," Rebecca replied. She could hardly take her eyes off him, but she forced herself to. He was wearing a thick cream-colored sweater, worn, slim-fitting jeans and a leather jacket. He looked so good, so healthy and strong. So handsome and vital. His thick dark hair was cut short, the way she liked it, and combed back from his rugged face. He wasn't using the cane any longer, and his limp was imperceptible. When he turned his face toward her, she noticed that the long white scar on his cheek was gone, as well. She didn't know why, but it seemed like a good sign.

"It's good to see you, Rebecca," he said quietly. "I've missed you. Very much."

She forced herself to ignore his words, to ignore the way his soft tone melted her heart. "Why did you come?" she asked bluntly. "I don't understand what you're doing here."

"I have something important to talk to you about. It was too important to tell you by phone, I thought." She looked at him and saw the light in his dark eyes. Her heartbeat quickened, and despite herself, she felt a flicker of hope in her poor battered heart. "Besides, I thought if I called first, you would probably hang up on me. Or refuse to see me."

"Probably," she admitted. Still, she turned toward

him and felt her heart slowly opening to him again. "What happened? Did your memory about the accident return?"

His face grew serious, and he nodded. "Yes, it did. But it's more than that. Quite a strange series of events, actually. What I've learned has changed my entire life since I last saw you," he confessed. "It will change both our lives, I hope," he added.

Rebecca's heart skipped a beat at his words and at the hopeful look in his eyes. She could barely breathe as Grant explained what had happened to him in the weeks since her departure. The Bentons, Courtney's parents, were slow in negotiating a settlement, he told her. Oppressed by the cloud of the lawsuit, he returned to his office on Wall Street. He threw himself into his work, but he missed her constantly, he admitted to Rebecca. He wanted to call her every night but didn't dare.

"I knew I couldn't give you the love you deserved until I settled my past," he said. "And when I sent you away, I doubted that day would ever come."

Without a settlement in hand, Grant's lawyers continued to work on the case, he went on to explain. They took a deposition from Grant's former client, Mark Weyland. Grant and Courtney had been visiting Mark's country house the day of the accident, and Grant had not seen or heard from Mark since. Mark seemed reluctant to give testimony, Grant told her, and Grant didn't understand why. After the deposition was completed, it became clear. In his testimony Mark revealed that he and Courtney had been having an affair and that she had called him from her cell phone, from Grant's car, right before the accident.

The news had shocked Grant to the core. He had been sitting at his desk late at night, reading the document, and suddenly thought he was going to faint. Alone in his office, it all came back. The night of the accident, the drive in the rain from Mark Weyland's house. He and Courtney had been arguing. She confessed to Grant that she was in love with Mark Weyland and planned to leave Grant for the other man. They'd been having an affair for months, right under his nose. Grant had been stunned. He felt as if he had been stabbed in the back.

What about the baby? he remembered asking her. What will become of our child? Courtney had seemed sad, he recalled. She hadn't wanted to hurt him, but then confessed that she'd lost the baby weeks ago. Lost the baby, and you didn't even tell me? Grant remembered how he had roared at her.

She had grown angry with him. The real truth was that she'd never been pregnant at all. Knowing how much he'd wanted children, she'd lied to him about expecting a baby, just to get him to marry her. She didn't really want children. And neither did Mark, she had added. So they were very well suited for each other.

Grant remembered how the rain lashed at the windshield, blinding him as he drove. He was angry and upset at her betrayal. But Courtney grew tired of hearing his accusations and demanded that he stop the car and let her out. Mark would pick her up, she insisted as she started to call him on her cell phone. But Grant wouldn't stop the car. No matter how angry he was with her, he wasn't going to leave her on the highway in the rain, he argued. He'd find a gas station or a store. Courtney's temper flared. They argued, and she finally grabbed the wheel and pulled, trying to force him to pull over.

"That's when the car went out of control," he told Rebecca grimly. "I remember it all so clearly now." He shook his head as if to clear away the unwanted images. "At least I know the truth."

"It wasn't your fault at all," she said, in awe at the revelation. "And all this time, you were thinking about the child, but there was no child."

"No." He looked down and shook his head. "There was no child."

She reached out and touched his hands. Her hands were shaking. He quickly lifted his dark head and stared into her eyes. "So you see, it's finally over, Rebecca. The nightmares are over, too. And the Bentons have dropped the lawsuit." He took a deep breath, fixing her with his gaze. "I have my life back again."

"Yes, you do," she said, feeling her soul lift in happiness for him.

"But I don't have anything without you," he added, staring deeply into her eyes. "I know I was horrible to you at the end. But I couldn't bare to see everything I wanted so badly just ripped away again. I didn't want to push you away the way I did, but somehow, I had to. I love you so much, it hurt every time I looked at you and realized I couldn't have you, after all. Please." He lifted her hands to his lips and kissed her fingers. "Give me another chance. I'll spend the rest of my life making you happy, I swear it."

"I love you, Grant," she answered simply, as tears choked her words and blurred her vision. "I never stopped loving you...and I know I never will."

Grant stood and pulled her into his arms. His kisses were hard and demanding. Rebecca clung to him, answering his fierce emotion with deep longing.

He lifted his head and stared deeply into her eyes. "Will you marry me?" he asked.

She nodded. Then finally found her voice. "Absolutely," she replied. How had she ever managed to stay away from him this long, she wondered as his mouth found hers in a deep, hungry kiss.

Grant broke away. "I almost forgot," he murmured huskily. Without releasing his hold on her, he twisted and reached into his pocket, extracting a small velvet box. He flicked it open with his thumb. "I bought you this hoping you'd say yes."

Rebecca stared at a sparkling square-cut emerald ring in a simple gold setting enhanced by small diamonds. She felt her mouth drop open but she couldn't help herself. "Grant...my God. It's beautiful."

"I guess that means you like it." He laughed, sounding satisfied that he'd pleased her. "Here, put it on."

He took her hand and slipped on the ring. She gazed at it a moment, then wrapped her arms around him again. "Thank you. It's gorgeous. I'll never take it off."

"Just long enough to put on your wedding band,"

he amended. "I once told you I thought emeralds suited you. Do you remember?"

"Of course." She remembered exactly. "We were standing on Fifth Avenue, looking in the window at Tiffany's. You teased me about buying me emerald earrings for Christmas," she recalled. "And meanwhile, I was thinking I wouldn't even be part of your life by then," she admitted.

"Did you really think that?" he asked, sounding amazed. He hugged her closer. "Couldn't you tell, even back then, I couldn't live without you?" He sighed and kissed her hair. "Now, we'll be married by the New Year, Rebecca," he promised. "It's funny how things work out. In a way, that lawsuit was a blessing in disguise. At first it broke us apart. But if it hadn't been for Weyland's deposition, I'd never have regained my memory. And maybe I'd never have been able to come after you."

"I'm glad you feel free of those sad memories, Grant. But if you hadn't come here, sooner or later, I would have come to you," she admitted.

"Would you?" he asked her. "Even after the way I treated you?"

"I know in your heart you didn't really mean it. I don't think I could have lived with myself without trying, at least once to make you see that, no matter what, we belong together. Besides, in all the time we were together," she said, realizing that in fact, it was true, "I never told you how much I love you. Wouldn't that have made a difference?"

"Your love has made all the difference in the world to me, Rebecca," he confessed, as his mouth moved slowly along the line of her cheek. "It's changed my entire life."

His mouth came down on her parted lips and she softly moaned. Very soon they'd be alone together, in a world of their own, sharing their love completely and taking each other to the heights of passion. Rebecca could hardly wait.

As she held him close and thrilled to his passionate embrace, she felt joy in her heart that he'd sought her out this way. But she also knew that what she'd told Grant was true. Whether he'd regained his memory or not, nothing would have kept her from him for much longer. They belonged together, it was an irrefutable truth.

The sound of quick steps in the hallway brought Rebecca to her senses. She looked up to see Nora standing in the kitchen door, with her grandmother following close behind.

"Nora…come back upstairs. Your mother and her friend need some privacy," Alice scolded in a hushed tone.

"It's all right, Mom," Rebecca said, learning back in the circle of Grant's arms.

"We have some news for everyone," Grant said, glancing at Rebecca with a secret smile. He released her and she turned toward Nora.

"Grant and I are going to get married," she told her daughter. "What do you think?"

She carefully watched Nora's expression, having a brief anxious moment that perhaps she'd sprung the news too abruptly.

Nora looked shocked for a moment. Then jumped

up, clapping her hands. "Yippee!" She hugged Rebecca around her waist so hard it knocked the wind out of her, then immediately ran toward Grant and flung herself into his arms.

Laughing, Grant lifted her high and enclosed her in a huge hug. "I guess you approve," he said happily.

Nora hugged him around the neck. "Absolutely."

"Oh dear…I thought it was something like this… But I had no idea," Alice said. She dropped into a chair and began to fan herself with the Thanksgiving menu.

Rebecca touched her shoulder. "Mom, are you all right?"

Alice looked up at her, her expression tearful and happy at the same time. "I'm just so happy for you, dear. I knew when you came home that something was dreadfully wrong. But I didn't want to pry. I was hoping that…well," she quickly glanced at Grant. "I was hoping it would turn out all right for you, in time."

Still holding Nora's hand, Grant stood next to Rebecca and put his arm around her shoulder. "Now that I have her, I'll never let her go, Mrs. Calloway," he promised, tugging Rebecca close.

Alice beamed. "Will you have Thanksgiving with us, Grant? You'll get to meet the whole family."

"I'd love that," he replied. "And you will all be my guests at Christmas, I hope. For our wedding."

Rebecca met his dark gaze, about to protest that less than two months was far too little time to plan a wedding. But then she looked into his eyes and felt herself lost in his loving smile. She knew that Grant could do anything he set his mind to.

And tomorrow wouldn't be too soon to start a new life with the man she would love for all time.

* * * * *

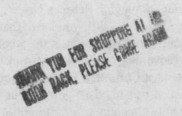

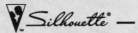

Silhouette® Desire®

presents

A brand-new miniseries about the Connellys of Chicago,
a wealthy, powerful American family tied by blood to the
royal family of the island kingdom of Altaria.
They're wealthy, powerful and rocked by
scandal, betrayal…and passion!

Look for a whole year of glamorous and
utterly romantic tales in 2002:

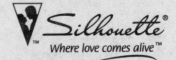

Silhouette®

Where love comes alive™

Visit Silhouette at www.eHarlequin.com   SDDYN02